King Camp Gillette

The Human Drift

King Camp Gillette

The Human Drift

ISBN/EAN: 9783742856609

Manufactured in Europe, USA, Canada, Australia, Japa

Cover: Foto ©Andreas Hilbeck / pixelio.de

Manufactured and distributed by brebook publishing software
(www.brebook.com)

King Camp Gillette

The Human Drift

THE

HUMAN DRIFT

BY

KING C. GILLETTE

There are clouds upon the horizon of thought, and the very air we breathe is pregnant with life that foretells the birth of a wonderful change. Darkness will cover the whole dome that encircles the earth, the storm will break, and from the travail of nature reason will have its birth and assume its sway o'er the minds of men.

NEW ERA PUBLISHING CO.
AMES BUILDING
BOSTON

Dedication

THE THOUGHTS HEREIN CONTAINED ARE DEDICATED TO ALL
MANKIND; FOR TO ALL THE HOPE OF ESCAPE
FROM AN ENVIRONMENT OF INJUSTICE,
POVERTY, AND CRIME, IS
EQUALLY DESIRABLE.

Google

PREFACE.

WE are rapidly nearing the most critical period in the history of this country. It cannot be denied, but it may be avoided or so met as to be of most fateful purpose in giving birth to a civilization that will be immeasurably beyond any civilization the world has ever known or history recorded. Twenty years will tell the story of irremediable disaster or of the triumph of reason. We are moving rapidly,— too rapidly for the government to adjust its cumbersome machine to the needs of the people ; and quick and decisive action by those in political and commercial power is the only hope that lies between this government and its downfall. All governments have fallen because of the insecure foundation on which they were built ; and this government is travelling the same road, to the same end.

Reform, with a pathway clearly shown that will meet and avoid the dangers which lie before us, is the purpose of this book. This pathway, once entered, will give birth to hope in the mind of every individual, of a future free from poverty, misery, and crime. Its final success as a movement would mean a more radical change than is possible for the individual to conceive, and would separate the civilization of the near future from the present and past, by a gulf as wide as that which separates the two extremes of good and evil.

The field of battle of this reform movement would be the commercial field, and the object of attack the underlying principles of our present system of production and distribution ; and it would oppose divided and competitive interests in the production and distribution of material things. I dispute the proposition that "competition is the life of trade," or that competition for wealth is the motive power of material progress. I not only dispute this proposition, but I go further. I affirm that progress, both intellectual and material, is retarded to an extent almost inconceivable by the retention of this element of chaos as a means of producing and distributing the necessities of life.

In place of our present system of competition, I advocate material equality; and, if my intelligent and analytical readers will have the patience to hear my argument to the end, I feel convinced that I shall stand shoulder to shoulder with them in a common belief and with a common purpose in view,— the purpose of launching this reform with a determination to see it forwarded to a successful conclusion.

I advocate the formation of a united stock company by the people, of sufficient magnitude to gradually absorb and finally control production and distribution, such company having in view the destruction of all tributary industries of the present system which do not contribute or are not necessary to the production and distribution of the necessities of life. Tributary industries include all professions or industries which are not directly concerned in the production and distribution of the necessities of life, but which are the legitimate offspring of disorganization resulting from competition. These include many manufacturing industries, many professions, and many miscellaneous businesses, such as insurance, banking, law, etc.

The necessities of life are food, clothing, and habitation. In securing these necessities, there are two great avenues of manual labor,—*production* and *distribution*. These avenues, when considered broadly and grasped as a whole, can be called the machine of production and distribution. Now, a machine which is built for the purpose of producing something, should be conceived and carried forward to completion with the one idea in view of producing that something in the best and most economical manner and with the least possible friction. No unnecessary parts should enter into its construction. In trying to mentally grasp and see in our mind's eye our present machinery of production and distribution as a whole, we are bewildered with the magnitude of the loss of time and labor that is continually going on around us, which is offered up in sacrifice to the insane idea, "Competition is the life of trade."

I advocate a system of united intelligence and material equality, under which system, the perfection of the machinery of production and distribution would be the constant and watchful care of the individual and collective mind.

I advocate a system where money and all representative value would be eventually done away with, and under which system, the manual labor incident to production and distribution would be equally apportioned to each individual without friction and with perfect justice.

The system of equalization of labor advocated, not only contemplates the maintenance in each avenue of necessary production and distribution of its required complement of laborers, but it allows each individual to select his or her own field of labor, and this without friction and with least manual labor possible in arriving at necessary results. Under this system, every individual would have the best and equal advantages of education. In material welfare every individual would be far better off than is possible to the most wealthy under present system ; and to obtain all this would require less than an average period of five years of manual labor in a lifetime, and the field of competition would resolve itself to competition for intellectual supremacy,— the only legitimate avenue of progress, and the true solution of the survival of the fittest.

The writer may be accused of an unusual amount of sentiment in his denunciation of the present system ; but, if all the truth in testimony of the imperfections of the system could be brought together, it would be found his judgment was founded on cold-blooded facts, and where a wrong is known to exist, sentiment is the first indication of a recognition of such wrong and the birth of hope that justice will prevail. A man is ripe for any crime when he confines himself to the unjust principles of the laws of our system, and shuts out from heart and conscience the appeal of sentiment and sympathy.

BOSTON, Aug. 1, 1894.

Book I.

THE HUMAN DRIFT

United Intelligence

vs.

Competition

THE
HUMAN DRIFT.

CHAPTER I.

The fourth centenary of America's discovery has come and gone, and has been celebrated with appropriate ceremony and general popular rejoicing; and the object-lesson has been one to waken the mind of every individual to the wonderful possibilities of man's progress in the future. It is only when we contrast our present material prosperity and intellectual position with conditions four hundred years ago that we begin to realize the enormous gulf which has been crossed. We can pride ourselves upon the advancement made and our present enviable condition as contrasted with that past; yet we must not lose sight of the fact that a continuation of that same gulf which lies behind us, still stretches out beyond the horizon of our vision in the future. As we turn our wondering thoughts toward that future, we have the consolation of knowing that with each receding year the base of knowledge will broaden, in consequence of which we shall be elevated to a higher plane and our condition improved. When we recall the grandeur and artistic beauty of the White City, its magnificent architecture and beautiful environment, and realize how from a barren waste it sprang into existence under the magic wand of united intelligence, we are impressed with the thought, Was it but a dream, or was it a revelation to humanity, to lighten the pathway to a new and perfect civilization and an environment made beautiful by United Intelligence and Material Equality?

The just solution of the problem of a social condition wherein aggregate of interests shall be considered anterior to individual interests, and yet based on the broad principle that individual interests and ambition shall have no unnecessary obstruction put in its pathway of gratification and free expansion, is still in an embryo state, and recognizable in that state by but few; but the gradual raising of the standard of intelligence is bringing us nearer and nearer to that time when reason and argument will take the place of precedent in directing our welfare, when we shall no longer depend on history thousands of years old to determine what our actions shall be in the present.

No reform movement can meet with success unless that movement takes into consideration the power of capital, and is based on present business methods, and conforms to the same laws. If a reform movement could be devised which conformed to all the laws which govern the commercial world, and yet be independent in its strength to all opposing force, either competitive or political, it would have all the elements of success within its grasp. Though in numeral strength it might be weak, it would have the chances of success of the individual multiplied by the number of supporters of the movement, and in such union of strength and concentration of capital it would be invincible; for gravitation in the commercial world is regulated by the same positive laws that control the material universe, and large capital attracts and must finally absorb small capitals and competitive interests.

The United Company spoken of in the following pages should not be looked upon as an individual enterprise, but as a system whereby the people would gradually assume control of production and distribution by a natural process of absorption. When viewed in this light, and its final consummation considered, as compared with our present chaotic system, it will at once secure the favorable judgment of all those familiar with commercial affairs, and carry conviction of its continuous success and final triumph.

If a movement is started from a single point, those who form part of the movement are those who understand its object and appreciate its advantages; but, if the attempt is made to accomplish by legislation the same end, we have all the conflicting ideas of society to contend against, which, on account of the wealth and power of those interested in the maintenance of the present system, would render the reform impossible.

I would not venture to propose a change in our present system, were it not for the fact that we have arrived at a point where the average intelligent individual can be made to see that the logical conclusion of the present system is the same that it is proposed to reach by the United Company, but the United Company would reach that end in probably one-tenth the time.

Under our present system the wealthy are just as much slaves to circumstances as the poorest beggars. They are under a constant strain of anxiety in guarding their property and keeping their surplus invested in safe securities. Besides this, they are mostly business men who labor night and day from early years to old age. They produce nothing, their only business in life being to so manipulate property that they may absorb the wealth which is produced by the labor of others. What do they get for all this scheming which is at the expense of their fellow-men? After all is said and done, they only get food, clothing, and a shelter, and means whereby to gratify their vanity and greed.

Under a system of equal justice, they would get much more, with less expenditure of labor and no worry or anxiety. Their food would no longer be adulterated and manufactured in filthy places;

their clothing would be better than is possible now; and their homes would be in a city free from dens of vice and foul tenements. They would no longer be surrounded by the dirt and filth of an ignorant and impoverished people, and no longer afraid their lives would be attacked by some despairing crank or maniac. Are not these reasons, in view of the fact that we are now slowly drifting toward such a condition of equality, sufficient to convince any one that the United Company, which has the same end in view, deserves the support of both rich and poor?

I am a business man,— not a banker, not a merchant, but one of that nomadic fraternity who are no less important in the complicated mechanism of commerce to-day,— a commercial traveller. And it is to this class that I am largely indebted, in their indorsement of my view that the drift of commercial affairs is moving with constantly accelerating force toward a common focus, that focus being the final control of the commercial field by a few mammoth corporations. In other words, the general per cent. increase in number of competitive individuals in any avenue of necessary production does not keep pace with the per cent. increase of population. As a consequence, there is a rapid increase of those who are dependent on wages, and a decrease of those who are masters or proprietors; and this, in combination with the rapid improvement in machinery for displacing manual labor, is the main cause of depression in business. Hard times are here to stay, and our intervals of good times must become fewer and shorter as the years pass. This must result in increase of poverty and crime, such crimes as have their birth in desperation, and send a thrill of horror throughout the world. Shall we wait till the dagger falls, or is it our duty to recognize the danger which threatens, and avert it if we can?

The manner in which the subject is treated can in no way affect the germ, or idea, which is this: That *open competition must logically result in final control.* Therefore, competition has within itself the seeds of its own destruction; for with final control of any product competition ceases. Further, that death to competition means centralization of manufacturers; and this means the dissolution of present cities and towns and the centralization of the people. Further, that death to competition and consequent centralization of people mean death to divided farming interests, and the control of production and distribution by the people.

The Stock Company is the most powerful and economical method of production and distribution in the world to-day, and under the law can capitalize to any amount, and control limitless fields in the commercial world. It differs from an individual enterprise, inasmuch as its continuance is not in any way dependent on the life or death of any single individual, but can accumulate and absorb indefinitely; and its perfect mechanism keeps pace with its growth. It is on this basis that the United Company is proposed,— to be unlimited in capital, and enter the field as an aggressor against all other corporations and divided business interests. We have in such a company the strange anomaly of the people as a whole entering into competition with themselves as individuals. We have the combined strength, wealth, and intelligence of the people opposed to individual divided interests. Can any one with average business intelligence fail to see what the outcome would be? Its success would be assured and its object attained when production and distribution had been brought to their most economical basis, and resolved into the hands of the people.

The fact that such a Company would have the economical power to destroy the present system of waste and extravagance is proof positive that such a Company is superior to it. Those who have objections to raise must bear in mind that "competition is the life of trade," and control, by a single individual or by the people, is the logical result.

Again, objectors can object; but they would be powerless to obstruct. The United Company is in exact sequence to a higher commercial system; and evolution in this, as in all processes of nature, shows economy and power over past methods. With every step in advance, what appears perfect to-day becomes displaced to-morrow in the light of higher intellectual advancement; and the time has now arrived when our present system, which fosters extravagance, poverty, and crime, must give way before the more just and powerful system of equality, virtue, and happiness.

My fellow-citizens of wealth and influence, I ask you, in behalf of humanity, to heed the multiplying sounds of discontent which comes from the masses. Like the low rumbling of distant thunder, it is the danger signal, which presages the coming storm. Ignorant humanity is as uncertain and as dangerous as the thunderbolt, and as unreasoning as the cyclone or flood, and can only be diverted from a devastating course by anticipation, and intellectual forethought.

These are times when we need unselfish men and women to come to the front, to pilot the Ship of State through the increasing dangers which surround us. Not a moment should be lost. A year may be too late, and the torch applied which will set the whole world aflame; for there is no disease which spreads so rapidly as the intoxication of madness which is the result of injustice and unreasoning excitement.

The gate of hope lies just before us, and beyond, a vision of progress, happiness, and virtue such as the world has never known.

CHAPTER II.

Never in the history of the world has business been organized as a whole in any country. It has always been a tangled skein beyond the power of man to unravel. It has been impossible to regulate supply and demand within reasonable limit, simply because every man is for himself, and he never knows what the rest of the world is doing. As a result, we have a constant fluctuation in prices of articles of consumption. At one time the whole country is overstocked with certain lines of goods, and there is a depression of prices. Then the manufacturers shut down or restrict the output, and the next thing we hear is that the whole country is short of these goods. It is here that the institution of speculation, or gambling in necessities, has its birth; and this lack of knowledge and power to regulate supply and demand, is, in part, the cause of our periods of depression and failure.

It must be conceded that every article of consumption must be enhanced in value in proportion to the extent of the plant necessary and tributary to its production; and it must surely follow that the total product of consumption must pay the interest on every established investment in the United States to-day, which includes every building and every foot of real estate held by private parties or corporations. The whole cost of running the governments of the United States, States, cities, and towns, and the salary of every public officer, and every improvement authorized by legislation, are a direct tax on the products we consume. Every factory, store, and office building is owned by some individual or corporation; and they look for interest on their investment. This, in the form of rent, must be added to lessee's expenses in conducting his business, and must necessarily be a tax which increases the cost to consumer of the product which he handles; and it makes no difference whether it is a grocery or life insurance, or any other business, it all resolves itself down to a tax on the products we consume. Can these facts be disputed? Is it not a fact that a grocer, along with all his other expenses of conducting his business, must add the rent which he pays his landlord, to his goods before he can look for a profit? Is not the wholesale grocer obliged to do the same thing? Is this not also true of all the manufacturing establishments which produce these goods? Is it not also true in the case of all brokers, agents, and commission merchants who handle the raw materials? Is it not also true that these goods, in their travels, must pay the total living expenses of all those who have aught to do with them in transit? The whole subject resolves itself down to this: that our productive and distributive system, if a system it can be called, is an unwieldy, cumbersome body, without head or brain, held together by laws that are a direct outcome of the chaos and disorder which surround us, and combining within its grasp seventy million ignorant, selfish, struggling animals that hold their glass of vanity up, and pride themselves on their humanity, freedom, and progress. Misguided, vicious, and intemperate brutes that we are, do we think because we have crossed that narrow bridge from a Monarchy to a Republic that there is no other bridge to cross, that the future does not hold something better in store than all this misery and poverty with which we are surrounded? The change from a Monarchy to a Republic did not materially change the method and laws governing production and distribution; and, as a result, we are gradually drifting into the poverty-stricken channels of European countries. It is only by striking at the root or source of the evil that we can ever hope to rise above the selfish and brute methods of competition.

There is no excuse for the existence of the extravagant plant of production as now maintained, with all its tributary industries, and no excuse for the continuance of disorder in production. The labor of production can be reduced to a small fraction of the labor now expended; and there need be no waiting to bring about this result, if a few of our wealthy and progressive men would turn their intelligence and financial ability in the direction indicated. The United States is full of such men. Cannot some of them be made to see the wonderful opportunity they have to raise this country out of the stagnant mire of crime and poverty, which has always followed humanity like a hideous nightmare in its march through ages?

It is folly to try to continue longer to gull the laboring classes with the idea that they are free men. They are gradually being educated to a knowledge that they are dupes, and always have been dupes, of a non-producing class. How much longer they will continue to bear this burden it is impossible to say; but their low mutterings of discontent will gradually rise to a volume of tone that will no longer supplicate, but demand, the honest and equable administration of production and distribution by the people.

There is no parallel between the working classes and the capitalists of to-day, and of twenty years ago. Their interests are no longer recognized as mutual. They are rapidly taking the position of opposing armies, and it is only a question of a short time when the tocsin of war will inaugurate the most desperate struggle between the opposing forces of capital and labor, that has ever been known in the history of desperation. History shows no civilization like the present. Consequently, it is useless to argue possible results from precedent. The wage-earner of to-day is not an ignorant boor. He knows that all wealth and progress are the result of his making; and he will not be content to bow for a much greater length of time at the shrine of speculators, gamblers, and thieves, who have robbed him of his just inheritance and the honest result of his labor.

Every human being should be free,— it is his birthright,— as free as though he were the only living being on earth; and the only object of society aggregates should be the advantages derived by each individual from the progress made by society as a whole. This would not be possible, were each individual to labor separate and apart from all other individuals; and it is not possible under a system of competition for wealth. With the absence of all competition for material wealth in a community, and equal material advantages secured to individuals, the basis of all contention that leads to poverty and crime is absent, and the freedom of the individual secured.

Under existing conditions there is no such thing as material equality or freedom secured to the individual; and slavery will better describe his actual condition, for no man is free. Men are born unequal as to opportunity and wealth, and many are forced into a condition of slavery from the start, from which there is little hope of their escape. Being forced into these unjust relations with his fellow-men, his natural abilities are allowed no opportunity of expansion; and the channel in which he might have found happiness is denied him.

CHAPTER III.

The United Company must not be confounded with so-called co-operative stores, or schemes to reduce the cost of materials of consumption to co-operating members. These co-operative supply stores have been, to some extent, successful both in England and this country; but they, at best, only save a small per cent. to those who participate, and the effect is not felt beyond their immediate circle. There is no backbone to these systems. They have not the power to affect the existing commercial system only to a limited degree, and benefit the working classes but little. Neither must the plan outlined be confounded with co-operative societies that have isolated themselves in districts removed from the rest of mankind. The plan, as outlined, contemplates a commercial war, inaugurated and carried forward upon the commercial field of the world. *It is the people combined under the smooth-running machinery of a mammoth Stock Company, against the people divided.* We must go further back than co-operative societies or stores before we can hope to dam the golden flood which flows incessantly, with increasing power, into the hands of the non-producers, the interest-takers, the schemers, and the manipulators. We must purchase raw material from first hands, and never let it leave our hands or give a profit to a single individual up to the time it reaches the consumer. When the people have done this, they have cut off every opportunity for the manipulation of material.

Under our present system of production, no man is secure in his position from year to year. From the laborer who receives but a dollar per day, to the railroad magnate who receives a princely income, the position of insecurity is the same. There is no telling at what moment the kaleidoscope of change in human affairs may sweep the

supposed foundation from beneath their feet.   Failure in business is
not a respecter of individuals, and strikes with equal indifference
those at the lowest or highest round of the ladder of fortune.   This is
illustrated by facts that come home to us every day in the failure of
men in every branch of trade, many of whom are of national prominence by reason of their large and successful operations in the business
world,— men who have controlled railroads, banks, insurance companies, and large producing and manufacturing corporations; and
even the fortune of a former President of our Republic was swept
away in this whirlpool of competition and crime.   There is not a single
branch of production that is secure for the investor.   There is not a
single branch of production that could withstand the onslaught of a
combined capital of one hundred millions of dollars.   The divided
interests of any single branch of trade would fail utterly before such
a capital, economically administered.   This is the position of the
manufacturing, jobbing, and retail trades to-day.   They are open to
the attack of combined capital in the hands of individuals at any
time ;   and, this being true, how can any one feel secure in any business venture with limited capital?   The fact is there is no such
thing as security in any business, and this condition is becoming
more obvious to men of intelligence every day.   It is estimated by
our mercantile agencies that ninety-seven per cent. of all men who
start in business fail some time during their life.   This takes into
consideration that some fail twice or more times; but, with the most
liberal calculation, it is impossible to figure out more than five per
cent. who are successful throughout their business life.   These
are startling facts, and show the odds against which the average individual must fight in his efforts to compete and be successful
in the business world.   Is it not a terrible array of facts, when we
see, with our mind's eye, this continuous procession of hunted and
despondent men and women who have made the fight, and lost?

Large retail stores are gradually but surely absorbing the smaller
retail trade, and the same process is going forward in the jobbing
trade and the manufacturing interests of the country.   These are
truths which hardly need argument in the face of facts that are only
too plain to the casual observer.   If the profits arising from this consolidation were secured to the people, there would be little to complain of; but the profits arising from any branch of trade consolidated
in the hands of individuals are retained by them, and the people
receive no benefits therefrom.   The result is the growth of a consolidated and compact wealthy class that is gradually narrowed down to
fewer and more wealthy individuals as consolidation proceeds, and
the growth of an increasing number of those who are poor and dependent.   The economic results arising from combination of wealth
in the hands of individuals would be the same in the hands of the
people, with this difference in favor of a company controlled by the
people, the benefits arising from such economic methods would
accrue to the people at large, and not to favored individuals.

The divided business interests of the country are a constant temptation to men of large capital, who find there the most promising and profitable field for their accumulated surplus; and there will be no line of trade secure from their attack in the future. In the consolidation of commercial business there is a wider field for combined capital, with a greater surety of profit, than there has ever been in the carrying trade; and it is only a question of a few years, at most, when this field will be invaded from every side by combined tens and hundreds of millions of dollars,— not with the idea of purchasing or consolidating present interests, but by the more positive, simple, and direct method of crushing them out by power of concentrated wealth and economy.

To illustrate more clearly the position of the retailer, jobber, and manufacturer, and show the insecure foundation on which their future rests, I will draw a comparison between present business methods and the method that capital would adopt, should it decide to attack any special branch of trade. I will take the shoe industry as an example, but the same argument is applicable to any line of trade.

If a combined capital of two hundred million dollars were subscribed to carry on the shoe industry of this country, with the idea of controlling the trade from the raw material to the consumer, cutting off every intermediate profit, there is not a tanner, a leather merchant, a manufacturer, a jobber, or a retailer, who would not fail before such an attack. Though the nominal capital of such a company would be only two hundred million dollars, their actual capital would be practically unlimited by reason of unlimited credit and borrowing power. Let us see what chances they would have over the present system.

Under the present system, hides are handled by brokers, who make a profit when sold to merchant. He, in turn, makes a profit when sold to tanner. The tanner makes a profit when sold to leather merchant, and the leather merchant makes a profit when he sells to manufacturer. The hides, from their first production up to the time they reach the manufacturer of shoes or leather goods, have been handled many times; and all such handling, cartage, and freight have been added to their cost. In addition to this, we have the divided interests of the different tanneries, warehouses, and stores, through which the hides have passed, all of which carry insurance on buildings and contents, and pay interest on investment in such buildings and plant. Then come the divided laboring class, salesmen, clerk hire, and the thousands of sets of book-keeping. All this must be added to the price of leather before it reaches the manufacturer. There are hundreds of large and small tanneries in the United States, and thousands of brokers and merchants who deal in hides and leather. The total income of these must be added to the cost of leather.

In the United States there are thousands of large and small shoe factories. These factories and machinery, including power plants, have cost an enormous amount of money, and are a permanent investment on which interest, insurance, and cost of repairs must be paid before the manufacturer can look for a profit: and to these must be added the office and selling expenses.

Some factories have their own jobbing houses. Others sell to jobbers. In either case, the whole expense of jobbing these shoes must be added to their cost. This item includes rent, or interest, and insurance on a very expensive lot of buildings, insurance on goods in store, office expenses, cost of travelling salesmen, their expenses and salaries, and general expenses attached to cartage, freight, and handling. Then, after all these expenses have been added to shoes, and the jobber has added his profit, we have the price to the retailer.

In the United States, there are, according to commercial reports, upward of twenty-five thousand retail shoe stores, which, if placed side by side, counting twenty-five feet front to the store, would make a solid block of buildings one hundred and fifteen miles frontage. The interest on this total investment must be added to the cost of shoes. Then comes the item of insurance on buildings and contents. Then comes the item of repairs on this total investment, which must be enormous, when you take into consideration the short life and poor construction of this class of buildings, and the average number that would have to be rebuilt from year to year. We next have one hundred thousand clerks and book-keepers, who must average at least five hundred dollars per year. This must be added to the cost of shoes. We next have twenty-five thousand families who make a living retailing these shoes, and expect a profit. Add this to the cost of shoes.

Now comes an item of expense that shoes must help to pay for, but which is not directly connected with the handling of leather, hides, or shoes. It is the expense of maintaining different branches of business that are tributary and contributory to the wear and tear on the shoe industry, and all other necessary industries. It is impossible to separate from the mass of necessary products, any one, such as the production of shoes, and calculate with any certainty its proportion of the burden of supporting tributary industries. It is only by looking over the whole field that we can obtain any idea of the frightful aggregate of waste of labor and material that is tributary to necessary production, yet is in no way necessary to it; and, if the reader cares to follow out the argument in his own mind, it will soon be found that necessary production, in no wise restricted in quantity or quality, could be maintained in very narrow limits, and the greater part of waste of labor and material now expended could be saved.

What we now say with reference to the tributary industrial system as applicable to the shoe industry applies as well to all the necessities of life. The tanneries, manufacturing establishments, jobbing houses and warehouses, and retail stores which are devoted to the shoe industry, are not built on the scientific fact that durability is cheapest in the end, but are built for present use; and security against fire or the destructive elements which cause decay is hardly thought of. The result is a lot of worthless structures that are a continual source of expense and labor to keep in repair; and their average life is but a few years at best, when they must be renewed.

This continual repair upon this divided and enormous plant of tanneries, factories, jobbing houses, warehouses, and retail stores,
demands the employment of thousands of laborers in brick-yards,
quarries, foundries, machine shops, lumber camps, lumber yards,
sash and blind factories, planing mills, glass factories, coal mines,
freight-car shops, railroad employees, book-keepers, clerks, and
salesmen, in all these branches and in all other branches that are
tributary to building, repairing, and insuring ramshackle structures.
Then, again, all these industries which are tributary to the plant of
necessary production, under our present system, are built in this
same unsubstantial manner, and must undergo the same system of
repairs and rebuilding, which necessitates a further tributary system,
which means more labor and additional loss of material. This, in
turn, undergoes the same process; and so it continues *ad infinitum*,
until it is found that *the necessities of life must bear the burden of the
whole rotten and decaying system, which increases the cost of articles
of consumption to many times their necessary labor value.* At least
ninety per cent. of the labor now demanded by our present system
has no bearing on the production of the necessities of life, except
that it is contributory to the whole decaying plant of necessary and
tributary production.

In addition to the above, each necessary article of consumption
must pay tribute to the maintenance of the insurance and banking
systems, and the office buildings of our large cities and towns, that
are full of lawyers, brokers, commission merchants, agents, and
middlemen generally. All these can be dispensed with under a
united system. After this comes the life insurance system, which is
a fungous growth; and all the labor which it demands, from the labor
incident to the building of its mammoth office buildings, to the labor
incident to the business itself, is labor and intelligent direction
thrown away, for it does not add to our progressive knowledge, or
in any way aid production and distribution. It is, like many other
businesses, purely tributary to a chaotic system. It has not even the
excuse for existence of being contributory to production. Again,
we have the intricate and endless system of law that has its birth
in competition for material wealth. Its very existence depends
upon the chaos resulting from competition.

It is these facts which will make the power of capital irresistible
when it attacks any branch of trade; and the above, though crudely
stated and only partially covering the ground of fearful waste under
our present system, is sufficient to direct the mind into the right
channel of thought, and show the contrast between divided interests
and extravagant methods, and capital, consolidation, and economical
methods.

CHAPTER IV.

A company organized with two hundred million dollars capital for the purpose of controlling the shoe industry, could own its own tanneries and purchase its hides at first hands at lowest market rates. The whole tanning plant could be located in one place. From tannery, leather could go direct to its own manufacturing plant, and the finished goods could go direct to its different distributing stores, of which it could have one in each centre of population in the United States. All of the buildings could be fire-proof and built in the most substantial manner that science could suggest; and there would be few, if any, repairs upon its whole plant, except necessary repairs on máchinery. Thus it would do away the tributary labor necessary to present system of unsubstantial and poorly constructed buildings. Such a company would carry no insurance, and no travelling salesmen would be needed or employed; and their power to carry on a cash business would reduce book-keeping to its most simple form. There would be no jobbing houses for either leather or shoes, and the broker and commission merchant would be shut out. All goods would be loaded at factory in cars, and shipped in car lots, thus reducing freight and cartage to a minimum. In place of the hundreds of wholesale and retail stores in cities like New York, Chicago, Philadelphia, etc., it would have one retail store; and in place of the thirty thousand or upward of wholesale and retail stores and warehouses in the United States devoted to the shoe industry, there would be less than five hundred. They would be in a position to sell shoes so cheaply that they could compel the public to come to them and pay cash. Thus one store in each of the leading cities and towns would be sufficient. By reason of the enormous amount of shoes they would manufacture and carry in each of their distributing stores, they could make a much wider range and finer division in shapes and sizes, and could utilize their labor both in manufacture and stores to better advantage. They would also have the advantage that all large capital possesses in the purchase of material, such as material for manufacture, and machinery, tools, buildings, etc.; and they could utilize their waste material to better advantage than is now the case by entering into other branches of manufacture where leather is the principal item.

Can any one who is in the shoe and leather trade read the above contrast between present methods and the method outlined for capital, and say that his position is secure from such an attack, or that he could stand such an attack if inaugurated? Capital can command the highest skilled labor, the best and most modern machinery, and, beyond all, has the power of economy, which is irresistible. If it is necessary to manufacture a given quantity of shoes to supply the demand, and a company of two hundred million dollars were floated, it must be admitted that they would do an extensive business, *which must necessarily be drawn from the divided interests now established;* for you cannot increase the demand by increasing output, and the result would be to decrease the output of those interests already established to the same amount as would be produced and sold by the new company. None of those who are now in the wholesale, manufacturing, or retail trades, need flatter themselves with the idea that they are so secure that capital would have to purchase their plant. No divided interest has a single individual plant large enough or strong enough to resist the attack of combined capital.

What is true in regard to shoes is true of any necessary branch of production,— the clothing trade, the dry-goods trade, and even the grocery trade, which capital could attack and control inside of a few years more quickly and easily than the Standard Oil Company attacked and controlled the oil trade. The sugar trust, now looked upon as such a powerful and mammoth enterprise, would be absolutely helpless if a United Company were established by the people; for the channel through which they now reach the people, the wholesale and retail trade, would be destroyed, and under any circumstances, they, with their enormously inflated capital, could not compete with a plant forwarded on a basis of actual value. Fifty manufacturing establishments, all centred at one point, could cover nine-tenths of all the articles on a grocer's shelves; and, with five hundred stores distributed throughout the cities of the United States, they could destroy every retailer and wholesaler in the business, for, when they got through with what they could control, there would be so little left that it would hardly be worth the continuance of opposition. It is only a question of capital, combined with economical methods, to insure success and control of any line of trade.

One of the largest tributary items which such large controlling companies would save would be the expense of advertising, which results from opposition, and which does no good except to increase the cost of goods to purchasers.

It would only take a few such companies to encompass the whole field of production; and, as the result of such companies would be to depopulate present cities, as they crushed out the retail, wholesale, and manufacturing business on which these cities depend for existence, the people would naturally gravitate to manufacturing centre. Thus only one city would result, as there would be no excuse or reason for maintaining others.

The plan outlined for the United Company is simply a business proposition, based upon present business methods, which carries with it the well-known truth that *large capital and economy go hand in hand.* If evidence were wanted on this point, it can be found in numerous corporations in our country to-day, which control the field of production in which their capital is invested, and make it impossible by reason of economical methods for small capital to compete. The United Company would not only have this same advantage of large capital and economy, but it would have a field of extravagance and waste of labor and material to work against that is beyond human calculation.

When we remember that the settlement of all countries, from ancient up to present times, has proceeded on the same general plan of scattered cities and towns and isolated dwellings in the farming sections, it is strange to find that under a system of most perfect economy and most rapid progress, only one city can be maintained on a continent, and possibly in the world; but this is logically true, and must be the eventual destiny of advanced civilization. Any one who will argue from effect to cause till they reach the bottom of this subject will not only find that scattered cities and towns result in waste and extravagance in production, but that such division and scattering of the people is opposed to rapid progress.

When the mind is in a healthy condition, the individual finds his greatest pleasure in association with his kind. It is not natural for him to isolate himself from his fellow-men; and this is one of the principal reasons why men gravitate to large centres of population, and why these large centres of population increase in size at such a rapid rate. Many would suffer the poverty and inconvenience of tenement-house life rather than have an abundance in an isolated section; and who can blame the individual for this? A man is buried long enough after he is dead without wishing to bury himself alive during his short stay on earth. The association of mankind in large centres of population (and the larger, the better), and their contact with each other, broaden the ideas and give a larger basis of knowledge to all; and, in addition to this, they come in closer contact with every step in progress of science, art, and invention.

In the United States there are upward of fifty thousand cities and towns. The cost of building and maintaining these centres of population is beyond calculation. The combined length of their avenues foots up hundreds of thousands of miles (Philadelphia alone having two thousand miles of streets), which are only kept in repair and free from accumulating filth at an enormous expenditure of labor and capital, from year to year. The excavating of these streets for the purpose of laying pipes for water, gas, sewage, and conducts for electrical purposes, is not only constant in old parts of these centres, for purposes of repairs and enlargement of systems, but is constant in new sections, to meet the demands of extension resulting from a growing population.

THE HUMAN DRIFT

Every nation in the world and every government of the past has been wrecked at the narrows. It now lies before the American people. Have they the patriotism, unselfishness and moral courage to guide the ship of state through this channel of adversity—

Failure means Anarchy. Success, Freedom.

MATERIAL EQUALITY.

CHAOS.

ANTAGONISM.

MAN AGAINST MAN.

SEA OF COMPETITION FOR MATERIAL WEALTH.

POVERTY AND CRIME.

INJUSTICE.

COMBINED INTELLIGENCE.

AGRICULTURE

ART

MANUFACTURE

HORTICULTURE

ARCHITECTURE

SCIENCE

ENGINEERING

MINING

EDUCATION

INVENTION

SEA OF PROGRESS

JUSTICE, ORDER, VIRTUE, HAPPINESS.

The Narrows

Above, we see the ships of progress guided by the power of united intelligence. Each individual embarks on the craft where inclination leads him and combines his intelligence with others to urge the ship forward.

Above, we see every individual the pilot of his own craft. Selfishness is the power that propels him forward and the whole sea is choked with wrecks of unfortunate humanity.

PROSPECTUS

OF

THE UNITED COMPANY.

NOMINAL CAPITAL,

ONE THOUSAND MILLION DOLLARS,

DIVIDED INTO

ONE THOUSAND MILLION SHARES.

Par value, One Dollar each.

Actual Capital not limited.

Organized for the purpose of Producing, Manufacturing, and Distributing the Necessities of Life.

BY THE PEOPLE — FOR THE PEOPLE.

THE
UNITED COMPANY.

We, the people of the United States, here assembled for the purpose of remedying the evils and grievances which now exist in our social environment, believing that all such evils have their final cause in our commercial system of competition between individuals for material necessities, and, further, that united action looking toward the final consolidation of production and distribution into the hands of the people, is the only logical and possible remedy by which poverty and crime can be removed, and justice to the individual secured, propose to form a Stock Company under the laws of the State of New York, in the United States, known as the United Company of North America, and will elect such officers and make such by-laws, rules, and regulations as will insure a complete working organization.

The object of this prospectus is to educate the people to a full understanding of the proposed Company and its purposes, which, when understood, must necessarily win the enthusiastic and honest support of every man and woman who believes in justice. In furtherance of this idea, we would ask each of those who may be interested enough to read, to also think, and to argue to a conclusion for themselves from the basis on which the United Company is founded ; and, travel what road you may, you will always find that they lead to the same point of economy and justice.

WHAT IS THE UNITED COMPANY?

The United Company is a proposed stock company to be organized "by the people, for the people," for the purpose of entering the field of competition in producing, manufacturing, and distributing, the necessities of life at cost. To this end, it will endeavor to control the production and distribution of all food products and clothing, from the purchase of raw material from first hands through all its necessary stages of manufacture, and its final sale direct to consumer. From its inception, the United Company will bring production and consumption into closest possible relation, and cut off every item of labor and expense tributary thereto, except those absolutely necessary to production and distribution.

HOW THE UNITED COMPANY WILL DIFFER FROM OTHER STOCK COMPANIES.

The United Company will be controlled by the people, not by an individual or a single set of individuals. The magnitude of the undertaking will preclude such a possibility. Further, *all stock will be non-dividend bearing stock* beyond a fixed guaranteed interest for the use of capital. Thus it will be seen that all stock, to all intents and purposes, will be bonded, and will be a mortgage to the extent of its face value upon the assets of the Company. The stockholders will have no inducement to increase the profits of the Company beyond a sufficient amount to pay the interest on their capital; and there would be no object in creating a surplus, for any necessary extension of business can be met by issuing new stock. Thus it can be readily understood that the people will get their products of consumption at cost of production and distribution.

The fixed interest charge will vary upon the different issues of stock, which will be divided into series of one hundred million dollars. The first one hundred million dollars of stock will bear interest at six per cent., the second at five per cent., the third at four per cent. Beyond that point, the Company hopes to obtain all future capital at three per cent. rate or less.

The object in making the par value of a share of stock as low as one dollar will be for the purpose of giving the poorest of our citizens an opportunity to participate in the welfare of the Company. Every share of stock will be with it its equivalent voting power, and a single share will entitle its holder to all the privileges that might accrue to the millionnaire.

HOW THE COMPANY WILL BE MANAGED.

The Company will be managed by a board of one hundred and twenty-five directors, to be elected by the stockholders at their annual meetings. After the first incumbency of the presidency, and all offices above that of directors, the terms of which, in all cases, will be one year, the same will be filled by the directors, to be chosen from their number by a majority vote.

The directors will have the power to remove the president or any of the other higher officers at any time by a two-thirds vote of their total number.

The salaries of the president, officers, and directors of the Company will be limited to five thousand dollars per year, it being the purpose of the organizers of the United Company to make all positions of prominence and trust, honorary rather than lucrative.

All officers above that of director, and all directors, will be obliged to give eight hours each day and at least two hundred and eighty days each year to the service of the Company, except for good and sufficient reason.

It will be the purpose of the United Company to advocate the election of successful business and professional men to the board of directors,— men of known integrity and honor and financial ability. When such a board is secured, the public can rest secure as to the result.

In the hands of the directors will rest the responsibility of forwarding the interests of the United Company. They will decide on all plans and specifications of architecture and construction, upon all machinery for use in the different manufacturing establishments, upon questions of transportation, etc., and upon all financial questions or extension of the business.

All business passed upon by the president and board of directors will be turned over to its proper department, of which there will be several, each having its superintendent and corps of assistants.

A BIRD'S-EYE VIEW OF THE UNITED COMPANY'S PLANT.

In its first stages the United Company will confine itself to the manufacture and distribution of those products which are a necessity to the larger part of our population. These will include general groceries of a non-perishable nature and all necessary clothing worn by the average man, woman, and child, such as shoes, hosiery, underwear, white goods, dress goods, furnishing goods, and outer garments.

The manufacturing plant will be located at one centre, and will consist of as many separate establishments as the products of the Company may warrant; but no single product will be included in more than one establishment. For instance, flour, of which the Company would expect to turn out not less than fifty thousand barrels per day, would all be the product of one mill. The same would be true of sugar, spices, baking powder, extracts, chocolate and cocoa, soaps, etc. Each will have its own establishment, built upon a generous plan for light, ventilation, and ample space in every part, and with room for any future necessary extension. Every building will be fire-proof, and built as nearly indestructible and free from necessity of repairs as possible, and will be supplied with the most approved alarm and extinguishing apparatus in the event of the combustion of any of their contents. *Each building will be designed, from the ground to the roof, especially for the work it is supposed to forward, and will be a geometrical part of the machine of production, and will work in automatic unison with the machinery it contains. The machinery in these buildings will also be made as nearly automatic as possible, not only in itself, but, where practical, from one machine to another in the different processes of manufacture.*

Each building will be supplied with numerous elevators of sufficient size to raise and lower a freight car, which will make it possible to load direct in car from any floor, thus reducing the handling of raw material and finished product to a minimum ; and railroads will have direct access to the whole ground story.

After mature consideration, it has been decided that economy demands the centralization of all manufacturing; that one branch of manufacture is so dependent on other branches that it will be more economical to bring all raw material to this centre rather than keep up an exchange system between widely separated points. This centre should be in the vicinity of Niagara Falls; for here we have a natural power far beyond our needs, and capable of keeping in continuous operation every industry of the Company, as well as power necessary for all purposes pertaining to the maintenance of a great central city, such as would be the natural result of centralization of the manufacturing industries.

From this central point of the manufacturing industries, the finished product of the Company ready for the consumer, loaded in the Company's cars, would be shipped direct to Company's stores. These stores, as now contemplated, will number one hundred, located one in each of one hundred of the largest cities in the United States. It has been calculated that the Company will reach in this way not less than twenty millions of our population. These stores will be proportioned in size to the population where located, and in every instance will be of sufficient capacity to accommodate any prospective business. The location of store will be contiguous to railroad for the purpose of facilitating and economizing in the handling of goods, and will also have elevators of sufficient size to admit of lifting of cars to any floor.

The cities where the company will establish its distributing stores, with their population, are as follows : —

Cities.	Population.	Cities.	Population.
1 New York, N.Y.	2,000,000	27 Denver, Col.	125,000
2 Chicago, Ill.	1,500,000	28 Allegheny, Pa.	125,000
3 Philadelphia, Pa.	1,200,000	29 Albany, N.Y.	100,000
4 Brooklyn, N.Y.	1,000,000	30 Grand Rapids, Mich.	100,000
5 St. Louis, Mo.	500,000	31 Syracuse, N.Y.	100,000
6 Boston, Mass.	500,000	32 Columbus, Ohio	100,000
7 Baltimore, Md.	500,000	33 Worcester, Mass.	100,000
8 San Francisco, Cal.	350,000	34 Toledo, Ohio	100,000
9 Cincinnati, Ohio	350,000	35 Richmond, Va.	100,000
10 Cleveland, Ohio	300,000	36 Nashville, Tenn.	100,000
11 Buffalo, N.Y.	300,000	37 Paterson, N.J.	100,000
12 Pittsburg, Pa.	300,000	38 Lowell, Mass.	100,000
13 Washington, D.C.	300,000	39 Scranton, Pa.	100,000
14 New Orleans, La.	250,000	40 Atlanta, Ga.	100,000
15 Detroit, Mich.	250,000	41 Portland, Ore.	100,000
16 Milwaukee, Wis.	250,000	42 Fall River, Mass.	90,000
17 Minneapolis, Minn.	225,000	43 New Haven, Conn.	85,000
18 Newark, N.J.	200,000	44 Cambridge, Mass.	80,000
19 St. Paul, Minn.	175,000	45 Memphis, Tenn.	80,000
20 Jersey City, N.J.	175,000	46 Dayton, Ohio	80,000
21 Louisville, Ky.	175,000	47 Wilmington, Del.	75,000
22 Omaha, Neb.	150,000	48 Troy, N.Y.	75,000
23 Kansas City, Mo.	150,000	49 Reading, Pa.	75,000
24 Rochester, N.Y.	150,000	50 Trenton, N.J.	75,000
25 Providence, R.I.	150,000	51 Des Moines, Ia.	75,000
26 Indianapolis, Ind.	150,000	52 Lincoln, Neb.	75,000

Cities.	Population.	Cities.	Population.
53 Los Angeles, Cal. . .	70,000	77 Dallas, Tex.	50,000
54 Charleston, S.C. . .	65,000	78 Sioux City, Ia. . . .	50,000
55 Savannah, Ga. . . .	65,000	79 Fort Wayne, Ind. . .	50,000
56 Lynn, Mass.	65,000	80 Duluth, Minn. . . .	50,000
57 Saginaw, Mich. . . .	60,000	81 Elizabeth, N.J. . . .	40,000
58 Seattle, Wash. . . .	60,000	82 Wilkesbarre, Pa. . .	40,000
59 Tacoma, Wash. . . .	60,000	83 San Antonio, Tex. . .	40,000
60 Hartford, Conn. . .	60,000	84 Covington, Ky. . . .	40,000
61 Evansville, Ind. . .	60,000	85 Portland, Me. . . .	40,000
62 St. Joseph, Mo. . .	60,000	86 Holyoke, Mass. . . .	40,000
63 Bridgeport, Conn, . .	60,000	87 Binghamton, N.Y. . .	40,000
64 Chattanooga, Tenn. .	60,000	88 Norfolk, Va.	40,000
65 Oakland, Cal. . . .	50,000	89 Wheeling, W. Va. . .	40,000
66 Salt Lake City, Utah .	50,000	90 Birmingham, Ala. . .	40,000
67 Lawrence, Mass. . .	50,000	91 Bay City, Mich. . .	40,000
68 Springfield, Mass. . .	50,000	92 Council Bluffs, Ia. .	40,000
69 Manchester, N.H. . .	50,000	93 Davenport, Ia. . . .	40,000
70 Utica, N.Y. . . .	50,000	94 Dubuque, Ia. . . .	40,000
71 Hoboken, N.J. . . .	50,000	95 Little Rock, Ark. . .	40,000
72 Peoria, Ill.	50,000	96 Youngstown, Ohio .	40,000
73 Erie, Pa.	50,000	97 Lancaster, Pa. . . .	40,000
74 Somerville, Mass. . .	50,000	98 Springfield, Ohio . .	40,000
75 Harrisburg, Pa. . . .	50,000	99 Quincy, Ill.	40,000
76 Kansas City, Kan. . .	50,000	100 Elmira, N.Y. . . .	40,000

$16,310,000

The foregoing list of one hundred cities contains in the aggregate an approximate population, as shown, of upward of sixteen million people; but, if the population of the suburbs and near-by towns of these cities were taken into consideration (many of whom would naturally avail themselves of the cheapest market), the aggregate population, who would be contingent to the Company's stores, would be more than twenty millions.

The amount of money expended in each city for distributing plant and goods in store would be in exact ratio of population, now calculated at $5 per head of population for plant, and $5 per head of population for goods in store, thus making $10 per head of population the basis of permanent investment in warehouses and goods in store in each city; or, for the total population of twenty millions, a total investment of about $200,000,000 in stores and goods. Thus in New York the amount expended for distributing plant and goods in store would be $20,000,000; in Brooklyn, $10,000,000; in Chicago, $15,000,000; in Detroit, $2,500,000; in Harrisburg, Pa., $500,000; in Elmira, N.Y., $400,000, etc., each city having a distributing plant which, in value, is in exact proportion to the population as compared with total expenditure and total population which the Company design to reach in these one hundred cities. The manufacturing plant at Niagara Falls, which would be built and forwarded on a scale to control the trade, would cost less than $500,-000,000, including stock carried. This, added to the $200,000,-000 necessary in distributing department, makes a total investment of about $700,000,000 to control these necessary branches of industry in one hundred of our largest cities. This amount will not seem large when you consider that the railroads of this country are capitalized at twenty times this amount.

The main building, or warehouse, in each of these cities, from which the goods will be delivered, will not be located in that part of city where property is at a premium, but be situated away from the regular business centre, contingent to railroad, and will be plain to extreme, not a single unnecessary dollar being expended in its construction. It will be iron framework throughout, and plain brick walls, without trimmings; and iron joist and brick will constitute the floors. All doors, shelving, etc., will be of heavy sheet iron.

In addition to the warehouse where goods will be stored and from which they will be delivered, there will be in each city sample-rooms, — one to every hundred thousand of the population of that city. Thus in Chicago there will be fifteen sample-rooms; in Boston, five; in Pittsburg, three; and other places in proportion.

These sample-rooms will be designed especially for the comfort and accommodation of the patrons of the United Company. No stock will be carried, but samples of all the goods which the Company manufacture will be attractively displayed. Each sample-room will be connected by telephone and telegraph with the central warehouse, by which means all orders will be transmitted. The city will be divided off into sections, and deliveries will be made in each section at regular intervals, on the same principle as our present mail delivering system, except that in the case of the United Company wagons will be used for purposes of delivery. By this system, deliveries can be made each day as often as once an hour in each section. Thus no one will be obliged to wait beyond two hours for the filling of an order.

THE UNITED COMPANY'S BUSINESS METHODS.

It will buy and sell for cash only. Under no circumstances will it ask for credit, neither will it extend credit to its patrons. In this way it will not only reduce the otherwise necessary labor required, but it will save that percentage of loss which is a necessary calculation where the credit system is resorted to. Further, it will be able to purchase all raw material at lowest market price by its cash payment system.

The executive officers of the Company will be located at the manufacturing centre. From this one point they will be in perfect touch with every branch and detail of the business, from the first purchase of raw material, until, as finished material, it is sold direct to consumer. Every sale to a consumer will be made for cash, and a full report of sales and amount of cash received will be daily transmitted from the one hundred different cities direct to the central offices of the Company.

The United Company will manufacture its own paper, do all its own printing, and manufacture all necessary packages of wood, tin, paper, or glass. In truth, every article sold to consumer, from the package to its contents, will be the product of the United Company, from raw material. It will do no advertising beyond issuing a price-list. There will be no colored or fancy labels on its packages, but plain and distinct lettering on white ground.

The United Company will recognize the fact that the present system of competition between individuals results in fraud, deception, and adulteration of almost every article we eat, drink, or wear, and it will be its purpose to rectify this evil by manufacturing goods of known purity; and every product of the Company will carry with it a label which will state the quality of the goods and the ingredients, if more than one enter into its composition. The people, as a United Company, would not submit to imposition in goods manufactured; and no individual will be able to derive material gain by such fraudulent methods as are now a common practice.

No travelling salesmen will be employed, and it will purchase the most advanced intelligence in every department of manufacture. The superintendents of different departments will be men of known ability and long experience in similar positions.

THE RELATION OF THE UNITED COMPANY TO ITS COMPETITORS.

The United Company will enter the field of competition the same as an individual or corporation, and will avail itself of every advantage which the law allows to attain success. *It will not attempt to utilize or consolidate any existing plants, or purchase the good will of any business, but will work absolutely independent.* It will take advantage of that theory, "Competition is the life of trade," and, like many well-known corporations, will place itself beyond the reach of competition by reason of its large capital, economy in production and distribution, and centralization, as opposed to scattered and divided interests. Believing that competition between individuals is the prolific source of ignorance and every form of crime, and that it increases the wealth of the few at the expense of the many, it would be the purpose of the United Company to crush out this system, and place individuals on a plane of material equality. In the effort to reach this goal, it will turn to neither the right nor the left, nor give its aid in any way to prolong the life of those commercial interests which would necessarily be destroyed.

The United Company will fight the battle, neither asking nor giving quarter; and with its central manufacturing plant of from two hundred and fifty to three hundred establishments, its one hundred distributing warehouses, and two hundred sample-rooms, it will stand alone against the whole system of production and distribution, which consists of thousands of manufacturing establishments, each with its separate machinery and power plants; thousands of wholesale houses; thousands of warehouses; thousands of brokers, commission merchants, and agents; thousands of travelling salesmen; and hundreds of thousands of retail stores. That the United Company will win is a foregone conclusion. In the face of economical truths, its success is inevitable.

The United Company maintains that progress in the future must result in the control by the people of production and distribution. It is the final logical conclusion of evolution toward a basis of greatest economy and justice; and the mind can go no further, nor arrive at any different result. It is the logical conclusion of unrestricted competition, and the purpose of the United Company is to forward this conclusion in the shortest possible time instead of waiting for the slow process of consolidation between individual competitors, which may consume a hundred or more years, during which time, ourselves, our children, and our children's children will be subject to the increasing crime and poverty that follow in its wake.

Seven hundred million dollars will control the grocery and clothing trade in all these one hundred cities and towns, and with that control will destroy them; for upon the producing and distributing interests being divided, these cities depend for their growth and continuance.

With the disintegration of these cities the population will naturally drift to the manufacturing centre, from which centre the whole field of production and distribution must eventually come under control. This conclusion is inevitable; for it is just as positive a natural law that production and distribution must forever drift toward the focus of greatest economy, as that water will find its way, by devious channels, to the sea.

The mighty flood of intelligence has been dammed up for centuries; but the veil of ignorance which held it back no longer has power to check the mighty torrent of reason which is sweeping over the world, and man will be the master of his future destiny.

The United Company will be supreme in the business world; and it will be a question of only a few years when all present avenues of production will be absorbed and the people forced to a position of mutual dependence, when it will become necessary to devise a plan whereby production and distribution will be maintained, and the labor incident thereto will fall with equal justice on the individual.

In presenting this prospectus of the United Company to the public for their consideration, approval, and support, we do so without one particle of misgiving or fear of failure. The benefits to be derived are too great to be lost sight of; and we anticipate the support of millions of our vast population, who will lend their influence and money to forward this gigantic revolution, in hopes of living through this most wonderful change and most exciting period of the world's history. But it will be a bloodless revolution,— the result of excitement and enthusiasm to reach the goal of freedom as soon as possible. Not a man, woman, or child, will want for the necessities of life during this time; and, under the power of willing hearts and ready hands, the wonderful city of the future would spring into existence like magic, the material result of the combined negatives of imagination and genius, to bid defiance to the most fantastic dream of the individual.

When $100,000,000 has been subscribed, the said subscribers will be notified by publication, and a time appointed for a meeting to be held at the Chamber of Commerce, New York City, Chamber of Commerce, Chicago, and the Chamber of Commerce in Buffalo; and the preliminary business of organization preparatory to the filing of the Company's certificate of incorporation will be consummated. The public in general are invited to participate in the Company's organization and future progress. Subscriptions to the stock of the Company in any amount, from one share upwards, will be received.

Let the American people rise to the occasion, and reason will dominate the world.

NOTICE.

Can you — yes, you who are now reading this — can you deny the possibility of the whole field of production and distribution being brought under corporate control, that corporate body being the people? If you acknowledge such possibility, and are in sympathy and accord with the formation and success of a United Company, give expression to your interest by filling out the certificate on opposite page, and subscribe for such an amount of stock as you may be able to control, always keeping in view the fact that no subscriber will be called upon to make his subscription good until one hundred million dollars is in sight, when the success of the Company will be assured.

Sign, and return certificate to the publishers, Boston.

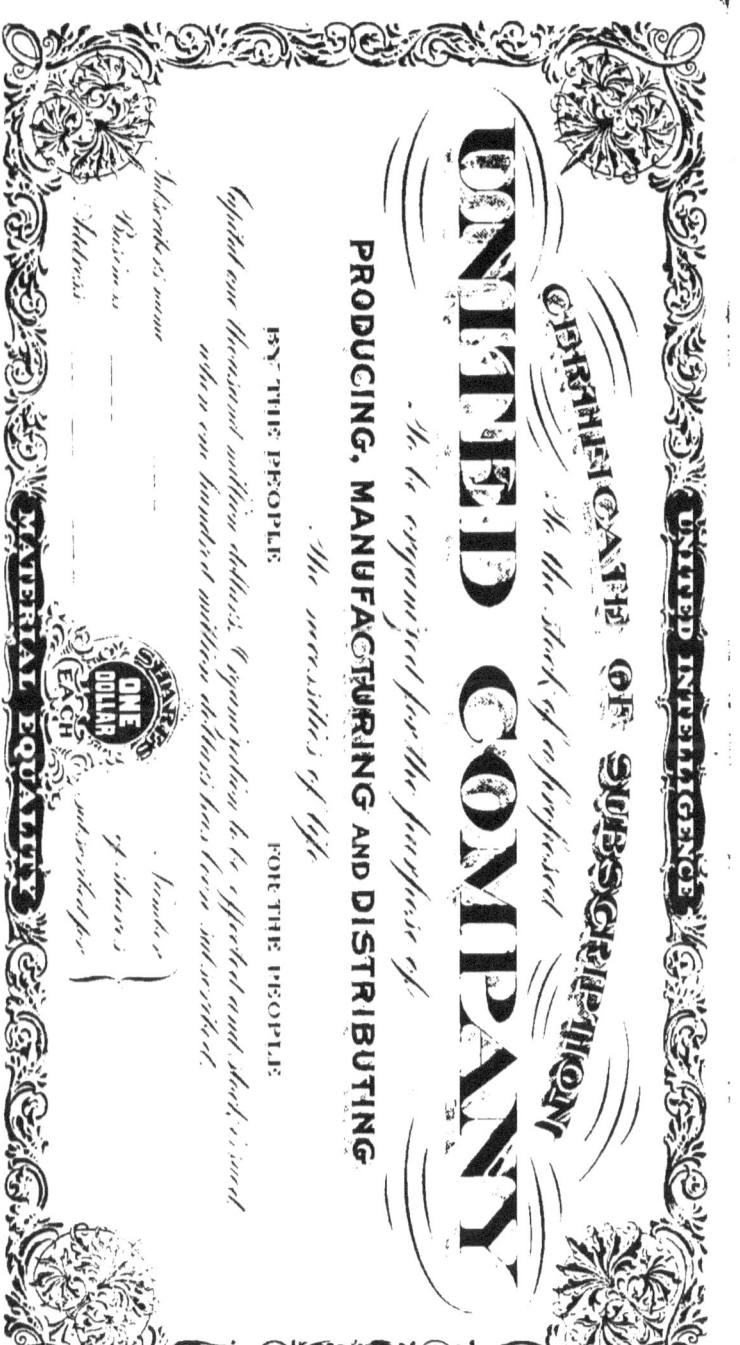

CERTIFICATE OF SUBSCRIPTION

UNITED INTELLIGENCE

UNITED COMPANY

PRODUCING, MANUFACTURING AND DISTRIBUTING

It is organized for the purpose of

the necessities of life

BY THE PEOPLE

FOR THE PEOPLE

MATERIAL EQUALITY

ONE DOLLAR EACH

CHAPTER V.

In the directing power of intelligence, are mirrored the shadows of coming events. These shadows may be but the reflection of an individual mind, but have the power to draw other minds to their objective point, when the shadows will become a reality.

Do ambition and progress depend on competition between individuals for material wealth? I do not believe they do; and, further, I do not believe the man lives who can give a logical reason why they should. Man must have an ambition,— an incentive that urges him forward. He must have the opportunity of winning recognition from his fellow-men. Otherwise, his life is purely animal, and becomes a burden. What should be the true incentive to ambition? Should it be competition between individuals for material wealth, which can only be accumulated by grinding the souls of his fellow-men between the mill-stones of avarice and greed, which is nothing more nor less than the compost which breeds the immoral germs of disease in society, or should it be that incentive which springs from an ambition to win recognition from his fellow-men for the services he has rendered in promoting their welfare and happiness?

A large majority of the people are under the impression that the incentive to progress lies in our competitive system for material wealth, but the assertion can be made, and logically maintained, that the great incentive to progress lies in the inherent progressiveness of the mind; and the whole mass of intelligence would, as one, take the direct path of progress, were it not handicapped in greater part by material necessity, which is made the basis of competition. Under our present system nine-tenths of our population live from hand to mouth. The whole power of their minds is absorbed in the struggle to obtain the necessities of life from day to day, which leaves no time or inclination to develop the mind by the acquisition of knowledge, its legitimate direction. The result is that the world loses the natural progressive power which would develop under a system which would allow of the free expansion of the mind.

There is no passion so strong in man as a desire to learn, when he has once reached that plane where he can appreciate the pleasure derived from the attainment of knowledge. All pleasures sink into insignificance when compared with this, and all other passions become subservient to it; but under our present system, when a majority of the people must give the whole power of their minds to obtain the bare necessities of life, this ambition is not only held in check and crushed, but in a majority of instances it is never born. The germ of this ambition to acquire knowledge and progress is in every mind, but in most instances in a latent state, on account of the unfavorable condition of environment.

A few centuries ago the plan outlined for the United Company

might have been impracticable, when man required the spur of competition for necessities, the same as other animals, to propel him forward. But now the situation is entirely different. To-day a large
part of the public have reached that stage of intelligence which
needs no spur, except their natural desire to learn more, and see
deeper into the wealth of nature's hidden mysteries. They cannot
turn back or be satisfied with inaction. Their whole happiness depends on further knowledge and pleasure which come in investigat-
ing and discovering the powers and secrets that nature guards so
jealously. Therefore, the time is ripe for a change. Nothing can
retard the future progress of man, after we once rid ourselves of our
worn-out system of competition for wealth. I claim that the people
have it in their power to place themselves beyond every ill that flesh
is heir to, and in a position of prosperity and happiness that are even
beyond the imagination. I further claim that there is no single or
combined power that could prevent this consummation if the people
would make an effort to gain control of production and distribution.
It is ridiculous for any one to assert that progress depends on a
struggle for material wealth, when the facts are that a man's mind
is not free to advance in the path of progress and investigation until
he has got beyond the anxiety and worry of material necessity. It is
then that every faculty comes into play and is under control. An
individual who once gets into the channel of investigation is never
satisfied to give it up, no matter how poor or wealthy he may be.
Under our present system he would be a fool if he did not make the
most he could materially out of his labor ; but, if there were no material wealth to be gained, he would study and labor just the same.
   Take Edison, for instance. He is probably able to retire, if he
felt so inclined ; but do you suppose if he were told that he could
never make another dollar from future inventions, but that such
inventions might be used all over the world, and give further fame
to his individuality, that he would stop thinking or working because
he could not get material wealth ? I do not believe he would stop
thinking or working if you would lay the wealth of the world at his
feet. It is an all-devouring passion of his mind which controls his
every action, and his happiness depends on the gratification of this passion. This is true of thousands of scientists, inventors, artists, and
others who have reached that plane of knowledge which, once attained, allows of no backward steps or rest from investigation and
progress, as long as life lasts. It is this particular path of knowledge
which is always looking forward that is the right path of progress,
and the one on which the human family depends for its material
welfare and intelligence. Life is too short to be spent in digging up
past history and relics of past civilizations; for the mine of the
future is too rich with promise of a true fissure vein to waste our
energies in the worn-out pockets of superstition and ignorance. The
mind must have an ambition, and, when you remove the ambition
to acquire material wealth, which now consumes at least ninety-nine
parts out of a hundred of brain power, it would find its natural com-

petitive channel in the field of science, invention, and art; and the attainment of knowledge would become the basis of our civilization.

In the immediate future, when material equality has been established, I can see a civilization such as the world has never known and never dreamed of as possible,— a civilization separated from the past in its every thought and idea. Instead of a scattered few of scientists and inventors who are handicapped by necessity, we would have the thoughts of every individual of our enormous population directed into these progressive channels; and, above all, they would be free from anxiety and care.

Children would be born to a condition of absolute independence, as far as material necessity was concerned; and their education from the start would be with an idea of placing them abreast of scientific progress, so they might all have an equal opportunity to win fame and honor from their fellow-men, and be of the most benefit to humanity. The whole channel of thought would be changed from a struggle for wealth to a struggle for knowledge and fame, and the rapidity of progress would compound in proportion as the base of knowledge broadened. Each step in advance would be seized upon by millions; and almost as quick as thought, another step would be made, which, in turn, would be flashed back to millions of minds.

CHAPTER VI.

That "competition is the life of trade" is believed to be indisputable, and is therefore accepted by many without argument. Now, if the life here spoken of means that we must eternally hustle, from the cradle to the grave, for the bare necessities of life, then I thoroughly agree with you that competition is the life of trade, and a mighty hard life's road for most of us to travel; but, if you mean that competition for wealth is a necessary factor of progress, or that it is a benefit to any human being, or that it is an economical means of supplying the material wants, then I take issue with you at once, and say that such is not the truth. For competition in the necessities of life is the root and final cause of all poverty and crime, and all the sickness and misery incident thereto. But let us look into this question of competition a little closer. We want facts, not theory.

I would like to ask my readers what the logical conclusion of our system of unrestricted competition would be. Has not unrestricted competition within it the final absence of all competition, when different lines of business are finally absorbed by centralization of capital?

If the logical result of our present system is the final control of different branches of production by a few individuals, and the eventual control of the whole field of production, why should we, who can plainly see the end,— when competition will cease to exist in every line of trade the same as it has ceased to exist in the manufacture of sugar and refining of oil,— wait for this slow process, which may take fifty, a hundred, or more years to bring to a head, during which time the majority of the people must submit to an increase of poverty and suffering, attended with all the horrors of increase of crime, when the people have it in their power to enter the field of competition, and within a few years reduce the production of the necessities of life to a mathematical and economical science?

There is no greater fallacy exists in the minds of men than that competition is the life of trade or an incentive to progress. It is just the reverse. It is the most damnable system ever devised by man or devil. It is the cause of every injustice in our social atmosphere, and is the only cause of all ignorance, poverty, crime, and sickness. By its maintenance as a system, the world of progress loses the greater part of its brain power; and the whole system is a waste of material and labor beyond calculation. It is responsible for all fraud, deception, and adulteration which enters into every article of consumption. It is a system of chaos which no man can reduce to order. It is a complicated machine which has a thousand unnecessary parts to every one that is necessary, and every unnecessary part is a loss of power and labor. No one understands its working; and it grinds out poverty to some, wealth to others, and crime indiscriminately to all. If I believed in a devil, I should be convinced that competition for wealth was his most ingenious invention for filling hell; but, not believing in that much abused individual, I must conclude that competition for material wealth is maintained simply through ignorance. Competition for wealth or individual power has been the basis of all civilized governments, and, by resulting oppression, the cause of their final disintegration or destruction; and no government can stand until material equality is secured to the individual, and intelligence and progressive thought are made the only basis of competition.

With competition for wealth, selfishness is born; for material wealth is not divisible without loss. But knowledge is divisible to infinity, and it suffers no loss; and the giver is made richer thereby, for it returns to him increased a thousand-fold.

Wealth can only be accumulated at the expense of human misery and suffering. The attainment of knowledge deprives no one of their individual rights or happiness, but benefits the individual and humanity. Under a system of control by the people of the production and distribution of the necessities of life, the whole brain power of the people, instead of being concerned in this insane struggle for wealth, would be turned as by magic into the channel of scientific progress. It is impossible for the imagination to conceive what a power for good this change would mean.

The whole world is an arena, and human beings combatants in constant struggle for existence. The gain of one is the loss of another. Success means luxury and ease; failure, poverty and despair. The weak are trampled under the feet of the strong, and their cry for help unheeded by those who tread them down. It is every man for himself against the world. Crime flourishes like weeds in a tropical bog, and finds its home with both rich and poor. Wealth is the material God of man. With it he can satiate the selfish passions of his nature, which grow in strength with its attainment; for selfishness is the natural sequence of material possession, the result of competition. Every crime stalks out of this same door of competition; and selfishness, war between nations and individuals, murder, robbery, lying, prostitution, forgery, divorce, deception, brutality, ignorance, injustice, drunkenness, insanity, suicide, and every other crime, have their base in competition and ignorance. Besides crime, ninety per cent. of all sickness is directly attributable to this senseless competition, such sickness being caused by worry, anxiety, and care, forced condition of living in crowded and filthy tenements, insufficient and coarse food, unsuitable and insufficient clothing, and forced condition of overwork and exposure. You can lay all this, and more, at the door of this wonderful system of competition. Do you still maintain that competition is the life of trade? If you do, you cannot deny its only possible logical conclusion,— the final control of production and distribution by one individual, one company, or by the people, the last being final, naturally; for no one will suppose that the people, as a whole, would submit to the dictation of one man or one company, unless such company were controlled by the people and for the people. This conclusion of final control by the people, which no logician can deny or dispute, means the total annihilation of poverty and crime and every tributary evil. It will mean further that material equality has been secured, and production and distribution reduced to an economical science. Has man lived these thousands of years without finding a pathway out of this mesh of poverty and crime? Must he believe, as many do, that poverty and crime are necessary evils which must always be with us? Then I say such men are fools; for a material effect has a material cause, and crime is a material effect, and its material cause is competition for material wealth. For as soon as you remove this cause, and place man beyond the need of competition for his material necessities, and on a plane of material equality, the incentive for crime would disappear, as though its very soul of selfishness had been consumed by the light of reason, truth, and justice.

What is it that fills our prisons, penitentiaries, and insane asylums? What is it that marks the face with lines of care, worry, and anxiety? What is it that consumes ninety-nine one-hundredths of the brain power of the people? What is it that fills the brothels and houses of ill-fame? What is it that makes you fear to pass through lonely and deserted districts at night? What is it that puts bolts and bars on your doors? What is it that makes extremes of poverty and wealth, that is responsible for almost all sickness and misery? What is it that gives ignorance to many, and learning to few? And, where ignorance and poverty reign, the crimes incident thereto go to the same cause. These questions, and many more, can all come under one answer. Competition for wealth is the base and cause of these defects in our social system. Every crime has its roots buried deep in this plague of society.

If half the effort and half the money that have been given to charity and efforts to suppress crime in the last twenty-five years were given to a United Company for the purpose of consolidating the production and distribution of necessary products, with the idea of eventually placing these interests in the hands of the people, crime would be a thing of the past in less than ten years. There might be a lingering viciousness in some, the result of hereditary development under an unjust system; but it could not stand the light, and would wholly disappear in another generation. Crime must have a motive such as our competitive system furnishes. With the absence of motive, crime would become extinct.

CHAPTER VII.

One of the universal crimes of our system of competition, and one which affects every individual more or less, is the adulteration of food products. The thief who murders us in our sleep is not more criminal in degree than they who wilfully destroy the health of thousands by these criminal practices, for the health of the whole people is affected for good or evil by every grain of food that passes the lips; and, if the public is imposed upon by deliberate lies or misrepresentation, and induced to consume that which is not what it is represented to be, a crime has been committed against them. This adulteration and these fraudulent representations in regard to food products are so widespread and generally accepted that the public have become indifferent to them, and are thus accessory to a crime which, though its effects cannot be always traced, are nevertheless always present.

The wholesomeness of food, and its absolute purity, should be the basis of its production; but these results can never be secured to the people under a system of competition between individuals, for the temptation to acquire wealth leads to adulteration, and it becomes a necessity, in some instances, to keep above water. The people can never depend on the purity of food products until they are produced by the people. Under these circumstances there would be no incentive to adulterate products. The people, as producers for themselves, would always strive for a higher standard of excellence. Thus all would be benefited by the change.

Under the present system millions of fathers and mothers, after a life of toil, hardship, poverty, and constant worry and anxiety, are made miserable in their declining years by the thought that they leave their children unprovided for. Can their religion, and the thought of a happy future for themselves, drive away this cloud of doubt as to the future of their children, who, left as orphans, are liable to be tempted to lives of crime and consequent misery? Any one who suggests the possibility of living without this grasping and selfish means of progress is looked upon as a crank, a simpleton, or a fool; but right here let me once again impress the golden truth upon my readers that the logical conclusion of unrestricted competition is control, and civilization must eventually reach this condition. My object is to show the people a means whereby they can reach this condition in the shortest possible time, and thus avoid the years of misery that must follow in the wake of a roundabout road. There is one logical result to be reached by civilization, and two solutions to the problem: the first, the one that is now going forward, the gradual consolidation and absorption of business into individual hands; the second, the quick and direct solution, the people to form a United Company, and enter the field of production, and as rapidly as possible assume control of every avenue of production and distribution of necessary products.

Under present government and laws, each and every individual is free to compete in the field of production and distribution. There are no restrictions placed upon the amount of capital a company or individual shall use, the amount of goods he shall produce, the method employed in the distribution of goods, or the price at which such goods shall be sold; and any effort on the part of government or law to restrict these privileges of open competition would be a blow at the recognized business policy of the world, and would meet with opposition from its combined capital, which every one knows is all-powerful when any encroachment is suggested against its privileges or rights. It is impossible, under a system of open competition, to say, "Thus far shalt thou go, and no farther." The natural growth of a successful enterprise makes it impossible to confine it within certain limits. Now, it is this established custom of an open field of competition where no favor is shown, and the well-known truth that large capital and economy are the basis of success, which suggests the idea of establishing a company by the people.

The rapidity with which such a company would change the aspect of the whole commercial world, and demoralize present values of every conceivable branch of trade, including the total destruction of real estate values all over the country, could only be compared to an upheaval of nature which destroys cities and towns in a single night. There is no one subject of thought which has a wider field for observation and speculation than this of consolidation, which always comes to the same focus,—the eventual control of production and distribution by the people, and with that control, the absence of poverty and crime. This result can be reached in less than ten years by the people, in probably fifty or a hundred if consolidation is allowed to proceed in individual hands. Which shall we choose?

Man flatters himself that he is far above the rest of animal creation, but the dividing line becomes insignificant when you compare the possibilities of man with his present condition. In what is man different from the rest of animal creation? The wolf ventures from his den to provide for the demands of his animal nature and the wants of his family. In supplying those wants, the rights of others are not considered. He intends to get all he can of the good things of this world, regardless of the pain and suffering which may result from his course of procedure. If he cannot obtain what he wants alone, he will join with others, and in packs and droves go forth to fight for it. Is not this also true of mankind? Each in his peaceful home, surrounded by his family,— does he not seek the same method of providing for the wants of his selfish nature, and for the wants of those he loves? Does he not go out into the world and fight for wealth? Each and every one disregards the rights of others; and unjust laws protect them in so doing. The law is the popular idea of right and wrong, which is nothing more, under our present system of competition, than a retention of the brute idea that might makes right. It makes no difference if it be strength of arm or strength of mind that deprives your fellow-men of their rights : the brute idea is the same. Man can never separate himself from brute creation until he separates himself from brute methods in supplying the material necessities of life. Like the brute, he hunts in packs. Nation is allied against nation; and in the commercial world he resorts to every trick and underhand method to circumvent his fellow-men.

When the people have the means in their power, and the way clearly shown by which they can force material equality, will they be so foolish as to lose a single day in putting this force in motion? No! When they recognize the truth, they will not wait for the slow process of government reform, the wheels of which can be so easily obstructed by the use of money and power; but they will begin in the commercial world, and work from the outside to the centre by positive means.

It is useless to argue the advantages of retaining the present system of divided interests. If it has not the economic power to shut out any possible rival, it must suffer defeat at the hands of a more economical and stronger opponent. When a system is once established which has within it the economic power to be permanent, then, and not till then, shall we find the ideal community government; and there will always be ferment and disruption from natural causes until this desired end is attained. Such an end has been within the reach of humanity for centuries past; and to-day we have only to hold out our hands, when we may all have every blessing that such a condition foreshadows and our advanced knowledge of production is capable of furnishing.

CHAPTER VIII.

At first thought, the idea of consolidating all the productive and distributive interests under one corporate body, or in the hands of the people, seems beyond reason; and so it would be if we were obliged to reconcile the conflicting claims of individual interests. But when these interests are all ignored, the same as though they did not exist, and we begin to lay our plans for producing in the most economical manner all necessary products, then the whole plan becomes simple, feasible, easy of comprehension, and irresistible. It is only a question of dollars to complete the revolution in a short time.

In the manufacturing and wholesale trades the consolidation of business in the form of trusts and large controlling corporations is making the most rapid strides. The Standard Oil Company practically controls the whole petroleum industry. The Sugar Trust controls sugar. Barbed-wire fencing is controlled by a trust. Then we have the cordage trust, the paper-bag monopoly, the straw-board monopoly or trust, trust for the control of the leather industry, type-founders' trust, etc. These are only a few of the hundreds of branches of business that are under corporate control, and the list is being supplemented by others which are rapidly following their lead. Such a condition of affairs was inevitable, and there is no legislation in the world that can affect its future progress. Why? Because if we enact laws which will make it a punishable offence to so combine divided interests, it will immediately open the way for a company of large capital to step in, in any particular field where divided interests exist, and by its power, and economy of such large capital, crush these divided interests. Then what have we gained? We have prevented the small capitalists from coming together and consolidating for mutual protection, but allowed the octopus to enter the field, and drain them of their blood.

You can make laws that will prevent all the shoe factories in the United States from combining as one; but you cannot prevent capital from entering the field in sufficient amount to crush out the existing divided shoe industry. Suppose for a moment that Armour, with his enormous capital and influence to command the capital of others, should conclude to manufacture shoes. In the first place, he could control the hide market. It would then be only a step to erect tanneries at one point for turning these hides into leather. Another step would be to erect a shoe factory to manufacture this leather into shoes, belting, harness, etc. One step more, and this same Armour company could establish its own distributing stores in all of the large cities in the United States, and thus retail direct to the consumer. They could thus reach millions of our population; and by selling for cash to small dealers, in places where they did not care to establish their own stores, they could reach our whole population, and thus command this whole industry from the raw material to the consumer.   They could sell at prices that would defy competition.   Who can deny the above possibility, when the concentration of capital in individual hands is constantly increasing, besides which there is the enormous power resulting from the combination of these individual magnates of wealth in corporate bodies?   If Armour to-day should signify his intention of backing such a company to control the shoe industry from the hide to the consumer, he could command all the capital necessary; and to consolidate and control this one industry would result in economical effects that would contract the whole field of tributary industry, and force the whole people to recognize the necessity of control of production and distribution by the people.

In the face of these facts, what is the use of legislation against syndicates, trusts, and controlling corporations?   It is only putting off the inevitable time when production and distribution must be resolved to a science, to a more distant period in the future.   *Instead of putting obstructions in the way of consolidation, every effort should be made to forward these conditions as rapidly as possible.*   I believe in any process that will bring order out of chaos; and this is the tendency wherever divided interests are brought under a single corporate control.   If you had a machine to build for the purpose of doing a certain work, you would put no unnecessary parts in its construction that would cause friction.   You would study to make that machine as simple as possible, and economical in its utilization of power; for economy in the use of power means economy in the use of manual labor.

What is true of a single machine for producing any article, is no less true of a whole industry.   If that industry is divided into hundreds of competing establishments, the people as a whole are paying an extravagant and unnecessary price in manual labor for the output as compared with what they would pay if those hundred establishments were consolidated into one.   Now, the question is, *Do the people, as a whole, want to be extravagant in their use of manual labor and create work for the sake of work,* or do they, as an intelligent body, desire to so organize and consolidate production and distribution that the maximum amount of production can be produced with a minimum amount of labor?   If they wish the latter,—and it is the only sane conclusion,— they must at once and forever desist from legislation that will in any way obstruct the natural flow of capital into channels that will centralize and consolidate divided business interests.

CHAPTER IX.

The economical results which follow the consolidation of any single divided industry are so far-reaching that it would be impossible for any other than an infinite mind to trace them. Thousands of pages could not enumerate them ; for, from cause to effect, they affect every industry.

Reduce a given industry which consists of two hundred divided manufacturing establishments to one, and what is the result ? You reduce two hundred power plants to one, and save not less than seventy-five per cent. in power demanded. You have repairs on one power plant as compared with two hundred. You have repairs on one building, which, if fire-proof and indestructible, are infinitesimal as compared with the repairs on two hundred decaying and rotting structures. You reduce the machinery required to less than one-third the aggregate amount used in two hundred establishments ; and, if you wish to run your consolidated establishment the full twenty-four hours each day, by the employment of three separate gangs, for eight hours each, you can reduce the size of your whole establishment to one-third the size in building, power plant, and machinery, as compared with the size necessary if you worked only one gang of men eight hours, as is the usual way.

In other words, a million dollars invested in buildings, machines, and power plant, in any manufacturing business which is run incessantly, night and day, year in and year out, is worth more than three millions of dollars invested in a similar plant which is designed to turn out, in eight hours, the same amount of product. The interest on the investment in the latter case is three times the amount it is in the former. Every time an improvement was made which necessitated a change of machines, one machine only would have to be changed in one instance, where three would have to be changed in the other.

Take the coffee and spice mills of the country. I suppose, taken together, there would be fully three hundred. If this be true, it is my firm belief that a single building, covering a ground space two hundred by five hundred feet, and ten stories high, would be more than large enough to turn out the aggregate amount of these mills, such mill to run night and day without cessation. In this case, there would be a saving of not less than fifty per cent. in manual labor in the manufacturing department. In the book-keepers, office help, travelling salesmen, and teamsters and horses, there would be a saving of seventy-five per cent. at least.

If this plant requires only twenty-five per cent. of the power formerly demanded for three hundred divided plants, the amount of coal to mine for this industry has been reduced seventy-five per cent. Now, if the coal is reduced seventy-five per cent. for this industry alone, it follows that the carrying trade loses this amount of freightage. This reduces the labor employed on railroads, and reduces the number of cars to carry coal. This, in turn, reduces the coal used by railroad, and thus reduces the manual labor in car-shops and locomotive works; and this, in turn, again reduces the necessary power of these establishments, and thus reduces the output of coal again.

But let us get back to the spice mill itself. By reducing the three hundred mills to one mill, you have dispensed with the repairs on three hundred buildings, three hundred power plants, three hundred lots of machines, and the wear and tear on many miles of shafting and belting. All these things affect every trade and business in the country, which are all so interdependent one on the other, that the slightest move toward greater economy in production and distribution is felt throughout the whole commercial field. There is nothing that creates a more radical revolution than the consolidation of those industries which produce the necessities of life; for all the tributary industries are in their most luxuriant and flourishing condition, like a lot of rank weeds, when these necessary industries are divided and subdivided into innumerable and widely separated parts.

Once let capital flow as freely into this channel as it has into the tributary industries, and there will be such a shrinkage in the tributary industries that the people will wonder that they have been so foolish as to retain a system which demanded so much unnecessary manual labor. One would really think that the maintenance of tributary industry was our main object; for, in truth, tributary industry employs at least nine out of ten of those who labor.

When the field of production and distribution is pictured in the mind's eye, divided and subdivided into millions of separate interests scattered broadcast over this whole country, it seems an impossible task to ever hope to bring them together to one centre, under a perfect corporate control. Yet when we say we will ignore all these interests, we will blind ourselves to their very existence, and begin to erect our factories to produce the necessities of life at one central point, and have our *temporary* buildings of distribution, one in each large city, does it not then stand to reason that these scattered cities and towns would fall like a house of cards, and the people gravitate to the central city? When looked at in this light, the proposition is purely a business one, and only needs capital.

This is consolidation, and it is a process that no power in the world can obstruct or retard to any extent. It is a condition of affairs which the people might as well face bravely now, as to wait and have it forced upon their attention by the gradual increase in poverty and crime which will follow in its wake. I believe in consolidation, for it is the right road to economy in production and the eventual control by the people of production and distribution; but I do not believe in the system by which it is being brought about, which is gradually but surely dividing the people into two distinct classes: the very poor, whose ranks are becoming more crowded from day to day; and the very rich, whose number are growing fewer and more wealthy. *This is the secret of dull trade and hard times which we see and hear complaints of all around us, and this at a time when the products of the country were never so plentiful, and the science of production at its highest point. The hard times have come to stay, and they will continue to grow harder as long as the people stand back and allow the present system of consolidation to continue to pour its wealth into the hands of individuals.* I said hard times have come to stay, and I mean it. The hard times will grow harder from year to year as long as the present system of production and distribution is re-tained. There may be spurts of activity and short periods of relief, which will naturally result after any excessive depression, such as has been experienced for the past year, from July, 1893, to July, 1894; but it is only a spurt, and as soon as the depleted stocks of goods resulting from depression are again brought up to a normal amount, and the country in general supplied, the depression will again commence, and each successive period of depression will sink the working and dependent classes to a lower plane of wages and a point of greater dependence.

In summing up the causes of dull times and these periods of depression, most writers seem to place little stress on the narrowing of the field of labor by consolidation and invention; yet these causes appear to me by far the most potent factors of increasing depression and hard times. And I think every organized body of workingmen should combine and amalgamate as a united political party, whose platform would be so simple and to the point that there would be no antagonism. Let them unite in a combined effort to establish material equality; let material equality be their plank; let it begin and end with this demand. Neither the Republican nor Democratic party will ever aid the workingmen. These parties are wedded to boodle, and are managed and controlled in the interest of capital. So why should any workingman give his support to representatives who only go to Washington to be bought and sold to capital?

If the productive and distributive interests of the country were in the hands of the people, every step in advance would be a distinct gain for all, and an occasion for rejoicing; but under our present system, economy in production means a reduction in amount of labor required, and an increase in the amount of poverty, sickness, and crime. The ranks of the unemployed are increased from day to day, from month to month, and from year to year, and every step of progress is accompanied by the groans and curses of the laboring masses.

Of what value is it to them, if, in a few instances, the cost of material is reduced by economical processes, if by these same processes there is a continually increasing number out of work, and consequently without money to purchase the necessities of life, even though they might be had for a few pennies? Every time a branch of trade that is divided into two or more establishments consolidates, it reduces the amount of help required in every department, from the clerks to the commonest laboring men. Thus a large number are compelled to join the ranks of the unemployed, and their chances of finding work are decreased; and this has a tendency to reduce wages, and increases the poverty of an already impoverished people.

CHAPTER X.

Consolidation of business is rapidly approaching that period when the people will begin to realize their position of servitude and slavery. We are only on the border-land of that wonderful power which is destined to change the whole aspect of the commercial world; and it is now, when consolidation of business interests is in its first stages, that the people should decide whether they, as a body, shall enter the field of competition and assume control of the production, manufacture, and distribution of the material necessities of life, or will allow the consolidation of interests to continue to drift into the hands of a few individuals.

The control by the people means freedom and happiness to every man, woman, and child, and the banishment of poverty and misery and every incentive for crime. The control by the individual means the gradual tightening of the chains of slavery, under which condition, poverty, with all its horror of misery and crime, will increase, and an aristocracy will assume control of every avenue of production, and own you body and soul; and the only escape will be through riots, strikes, and civil war.

What slavery could be worse than this constant slavery of the mind to an endless struggle for existence, which finds rest only in the grave? The slaves in the South were in paradise compared with the position of those who will be dependent on the masters of the future. Every slave in the South had a value to his master, and was consequently cared for; but the slaves of the future will exceed the demand, and many will be compelled to live in poverty and want. Which is to be preferred, to be a slave and be fed, clothed, and housed, or be a slave and depend on chance for the necessities of life? I know what the answer will be to this from a majority of the people. In the latter case they will say that man has the opportunity to rise, and get above a position of dependence and slavery. This is true; but it does not get around the fact that there is an ever-constant number who are in this position of slavery, and this number is bound to increase as consolidation in the hands of individuals proceeds.

Was it not wonderful how the people of the North were roused to enthusiasm which freed the slaves of the South? Was it not wonderful how millions took up arms and risked their lives, when they realized the injustice of human bondage? Now, here around us all, is a slavery that is worse in every way and more far-reaching in its effect than was the slavery of the South. There is no escape for the slaves of to-day. Misery and poverty of mind and body follow them wherever they go, and the spur of adversity and want is more painful than the cat-o'-nine-tails of the South. Cannot the people be once more roused to enthusiasm in the interest of humanity,— not a part of humanity, but the whole of humanity? It requires no war, no bloodshed, no misery, to follow in the wake of this revolution, and the result would be the emancipation of the human mind and body from want, poverty, crime, and sickness, and the inauguration of freedom and happiness forever; and this could be brought about for less than half the cost in money of the late Civil War.

The prediction of the future condition of the people is not overdrawn, for, if the past twenty years, and the present, are any indication of that future, the horror and crime of that future are not half told; and it will be the intelligent and educated people who will be responsible for the effect. Strikes, riots, incendiary mobs, and secret orders of anarchists, socialists, and revolutionists, will make the lives of public and wealthy individuals the mark for their wrath resulting from despair, destitution, and want; and the wealthy will live in constant fear and terror of every poorly dressed individual they meet. It is only necessary to read the despatches from all over the world that fill our daily papers, which record the acts of violence of the dependent classes, to be convinced that their desperation is becoming more and more a menace to existing institutions. Is there any excuse for clinging to a system which leads to a constant increase in such acts of violence resulting from desperation; or is there any pleasure in hoarding up wealth at the price of your own safety and welfare?

He who has a grain of sense, must see that at the present rate of consolidation and improvement in labor-saving machinery, such a thing as good times to the lower or middle classes can never come again under our present system. We try to give the reason for this continued depression. At one time it is said to be political agitation; another, overproduction; another, short crops; another, no foreign demand, etc. But the real reason is that our whole system of production and distribution is radically wrong and beyond comprehension as to its extravagance and waste, on top of which come consolidation of business and improvement in labor-saving machinery, which continually increase the number of the unemployed. This reason, the only reason, is hardly ever touched upon. We accept our system as the only one possible, boast of our progress and freedom, and this while we are living in the most abject state of slavery. Can you show me one who is not a slave to this competitive system between individuals? We are all, like hyenas in a cage, watching an opportunity to fly at each other's throats. The rich man is a slave to his money; his whole mind is occupied with its care and the fear of losing it; while the poor man is a slave to his actual necessities.

The mass of the people are ignorant, and cannot see beyond the present effect of consolidation; and to see a single corporation spring into existence which proposes to crush out cities and towns, and close forever the millions of wholesale and retail stores, manufacturing establishments, and various branches of trade, and which is to deprive hundreds of thousands of that employment which has been their means of livlihood, will make them raise their voices in an agony of protestation as they watch the destruction. They are, and will be, too thick-headed to appreciate the fact that this revolution is brought about by economy. The very fact that it can destroy the present system is evidence that it is superior to it; and, if the result of this change, this economy in production, can eventually accrue to the people at large, they can well afford to see an end of the present system. During the whole change from one system to the other, which could be accomplished in a few years, there would be no necessity for man, woman, or child to suffer from material want.

During the gradual progress of the United Company in its absorption of the fields of production and the centralization of the manufacturing industries, there would be a vast number of people thrown out of employment. These people could all be employed by the government in the building of the great central city, "Metropolis." Would it not be just as legitimate for the government to employ five millions of people in this great constructive undertaking as it was to employ three millions of men in a war of destruction, as was the case during the Civil War?

Since the beginning of history, we find in every age, the recorded efforts of so-called reformers,—men and women who have given their every effort and sacrificed their lives in the hope of bettering the condition of mankind. They knew and felt that there was something radically wrong in systems which fostered poverty and wealth side by side. The failures of these reform movements were mainly due to the fact that the reformers themselves failed to understand the causes of the evils which they sought to remedy, and were therefore unable to outline a plan of proceeding which would clearly show the beginning and end. Failing in this most vital point, they could not hope to gain the co-operation and confidence of the public. Then, again, failure resulted from the fact that the plans advocated required legislation and support of a majority of the people; and, where diversity of interest was so great, it was impossible to gain the support of any but those who had nothing to lose, and this class, no matter how numerous, have always been helpless in the hands of money and power.

The plan of reform advocated in this book differs from others. It shows a well-defined path from beginning to end; and, rightly considered, the change would be as great a benefit to those who are wealthy as to the poor. The plan does not need the support of a majority of the people, but could be forwarded and made a success against all opposition, if supported by a few. Neither does it need the sanction of the government or any special legislation in its behalf. Women would count the same as men, and their active interest and support would be as valuable; while the success of the movement would mean to woman such freedom and happiness as has never been dreamed of by the most ardent advocates of women's rights.

The benefit to women which would result from the success of the United Company is an argument in its favor which should not be lost sight of. With its final triumph, women, for the first time in history, would be free, sharing with equal right the material benefits derived from progress, and no longer restricted by laws to a limited field of action.

Can any of my readers realize what this means to women,— this equal right with men to material welfare, this independence which would deprive marriage of every mercenary motive ? It means the emancipation of more than half the human race from a degrading and inferior bondage which had been forced upon them and held them down through centuries. Women have it in their power to forward this movement and make it a success. They have the inborn sympathy and unselfish courage to discard individual interest in the pursuit of any great and common object for humanity's welfare. If woman really desires her freedom and emancipation from the degrading position which has always been her lot in her relations with man, the opportunity is hers by aiding to forward this United Company.

The most that woman can hope for as long as the present system exists, is a slow recognition of the rights they demand. With the success of the United Company, they would be placed on the same plane as men, at once and forever.

To those of education and wealth, who may be disposed to withhold their support of this movement from a fear of being brought to a level with the common herd of humanity, I would say this : The future, under our present system, is always uncertain for the individual ; and, though you may be happy and secure in your position to-day, you may be one of the unfortunates of society to-morrow, or, if not yourself, your children may be brought to poverty and crime in another generation. Would it not be better to support a movement that would evolve a system which would allow you to die with the conviction that the future welfare of your children was secure, rather than cling to a system, from selfish motives, which must necessarily fill the mind of every mother and father with uncertainty, when they try to picture the future of those they have brought into the world and love ? Can any one who has a heart and soul that is true to nature, hesitate ?

They of the present generation will soon pass away, and in their place will rise their children. None can look far enough ahead to map out their children's lives. Their lines may fall in pleasant places, where, free from temptations that rise from poverty and want, goodness and virtue may guide their footsteps, or their pathway may be a living agony, strewn with thorns of sorrow, poverty, and crime.

With this uncertainty of the future, who would wish to retain the shifting kaleidoscope of competition? The chances of success and happiness under our system — and it matters not how bright or clever the individual may be — are less than the chances of drawing a prize in a lottery; and truth and virtue are not the necessary factors to success.

It is true that under this reform movement you would eventually be brought with others to a common level, as far as material equality was concerned; but, with the absence of poverty and incentive for crime, a generation would work a wonderful change in humanity. There would be no longer a common herd. And you must further remember that in the future, as now, mankind can choose his own friends and associates.

I would like to ask that class who arrogate to themselves all the benefits derived from the progress of science, art, and invention, and who relegate the rest of mankind to a condition of servitude that has not been materially improved since the dark ages, by what right they claim these special privileges? Do they claim them under a moral law, or under those laws which govern the social and commercial world? The moral law is the conscious law of the individual mind which distinguishes right from wrong.

In this evenly balanced scale of justice and truth, selfishness will be found to weigh down these claims to special privileges; and selfishness is not only a crime, but it is the father of all crimes and acts of injustice. On the other hand, if you claim these special privileges under the laws which govern the social and commercial world, which recognizes competition as the basis of progress and individual success, to which you can directly attribute your present position, you cannot reasonably oppose or object to a United Company, by the people, which would be organized and carried forward under these same laws, with this difference in favor of the establishment of a United Company,— that, while recognizing and respecting those laws, it would go a step farther, and recognize the moral law of right of each and every individual to equal material benefits derived from progress, and equal educational advantages. *The equal right of individuals to the products of nature and the benefits derived from progress, is based upon the fact that the ever-present progressive condition of mankind is founded upon the efforts of all past generations, and not upon present individual effort. Man only builds upon the foundation of accumulated intelligence, and has no moral right to claim special privileges for himself from the benefits arising from this foundation of thought, which is an inheritance to humanity at large, and should descend with equal justice to every individual.*

It is the struggle for the necessities of life which imbitters our existence. Not one in a hundred of our population is free from a chronic state of anxiety, and not without reason; for his inability to save, in this hand-to-mouth existence, keeps before him the skeleton of want in the future, when from sickness or old age he is unable longer to struggle.

CHAPTER XI.

Under a system of material equality, money would resolve itself to a simple form, and eventually pass out of existence entirely. This is just as true as that the sun rises and sets, and less than fifty years would see such conditions firmly established in all North America. It is useless to dig up the past to disprove this. The past has no parallel with the present progressive position or average intelligence of mankind. At no time, up to the present century, has the direct path of progress been recognized. Every civilization has been looking for a light to guide them out of the labyrinth of poverty, crime, and superstition with which they were surrounded. Government after government was born and raised, only to totter and fall because of its false and insecure foundation; and no government in the world will ever stand until material equality has been secured to the individual. When such a basis is secured, the Rock of Ages itself will not be more firm on its foundation than the progress and happiness of mankind.

With the disappearance of money, the people, as a whole, will be the father of the individual, and stand in the same relation to each and every individual as a good father stands in relation to his children. Every material want will be gratified, without question, without price. Would the people abuse this privilege? No, no more than a good child abuses the love and confidence of his parents.

It will be argued by many that if unrestricted license were given to the public in the supply of their material wants, they would abuse this privilege, and go to excess in their demands. Such might be the case if we had the people of the present civilization to deal with, with their hereditary and strongly developed ideas of property and personal display; but, with the gradual change of our present system to one of material equality, civilization itself would undergo a wonderful change in its ideas.

With the absence of competition and the incentive to accumulate property by the individual, and his absolute independence as far as his material necessities were concerned, there would be also an absence of material selfishness and desire to make an envious display of wealth. Any one trying to make such display by infringing upon the public treasury beyond the established custom of reasonable latitude and liberality, instead of exciting the envy of his or her friends or associates, would be a subject for their derision and contempt.

There would be no necessity for any individual to accumulate beyond his immediate necessities; for the public treasury would always be at hand to draw from to meet his requirements, and any extravagant use or destruction of material would only result in an increased demand on labor of production. This would not only be a recognized and ever-present reminder of economical use of the products of labor, but would be the keystone of economy; and, though the foundation of progress would demand abundance of highest grade of product, yet the principle of economy in the use of this product would never be lost sight of by the individual.

No one who is acquainted with our present progressive position, and the possibilities of production under an economical system, will deny that we have it in our power to produce all that the most extravagant mind could devise, and give to each and every individual more than the most favored individual under our present system can hope to attain or purchase with his wealth. And this can be done with less than one-tenth the labor now in the field of production. You who protest against consolidation and united intelligence, what do you want? Can you not be satisfied with every material want gratified, and your mind given its freedom? Must you gratify your selfish greed by upholding a system which gives you power to grind your fellow-men in poverty and crime? Have you developed on the lines of selfishness to that point where every good and natural impulse of the mind is crushed, and conscience dead?

Is it not possible, and is it not time, that the mind should rise above the struggle for material wealth? Is it not a higher plane of competition for the mind to develop science than to devote one's brains for life to the accumulation of wealth?

Under a system of material equality and non-recognition of value, law, as we understand it to-day, would have little place; for law, in greater part, relates to property rights, and it is this recognition of property rights that makes it possible for crime to be so widespread. Place individuals on a plane of material equality, and the cause of nine-tenths of all crimes will disappear.

The great mistake of the average individual is to give a snap-judgment on almost every proposition of reform; and, when a possibility of material equality is suggested, he fails to see the force of conclusions by which man would adjust himself to those conditions. Man always adjusts himself to environment, and it would be easier to adjust himself to a condition where there would be no poverty or incentive for crime, than it is to adjust himself to conditions where every individual must struggle against all other individuals for existence.

If poverty can be removed, and ninety-five per cent. of crime wiped out by establishing material equality, no other argument should be necessary to get the enthusiastic support of every human being.

Just so long as the present individual competitive commercial system of production and distribution continues, poverty, with all its horror of crime and misery, will still surround us. In this respect, we have made no perceptible advance in a thousand years, during which time, the necessity for manual labor for a given amount of production has been reduced by progress in science and invention to less than one one-hundredth part.

Is it possible that there can be men and women so low and self-ish that they can look down from their supposed position of secu-rity and wealth, and not desire the establishment of a system that will remove poverty and crime and bring happiness to all? The apparent injustice of individual welfare is a condition, and it is within the power of the people to change that condition to one of equal justice.

The shifting sands of Father Time work unforeseen changes in the fortunes of men, and the children of the rich men to-day may be com-pelled to labor for the poor man's child in another generation. It is for this reason that a change which will insure the welfare and happi-ness of all should be the desire of the rich and influential of to-day. If this class would use their wealth and influence to forward the United Company, they would be sure of the future welfare of their children,— a future far in advance of what they could hope to secure from individual wealth.

My task has been to point out a pathway, broad and straight be-fore us, ready to enter. This path leads direct to a future beyond the ideal imagination of the most imaginative,— a pathway of econ-omy, which, if once entered, will revolutionize the world, and divide man from brute creation through all future time.

I appeal to those who believe in the practical application of this system of reform to put some life and action in their belief. Those who are unable to financially support a company, let them agitate the question wherever and whenever they can, argue the question until the last vestige of opposition is swept away by the truth, write for papers, write for magazines, and write books,— do anything that will educate the people up to the advantages to be derived by them-selves and by their children when production and distribution are in the hands of the people. If a debate were inaugurated throughout the United States in every home, in every society, in every church, in every school, and factory, and industrial establishment, on the one question,— Resolved, Do crime and poverty result solely from our competitive commercial system?— I am convinced the final con-clusion would be a universal affirmative answer; for it seems impos-sible to arrive at any other conclusion. Then, if a companion ques-tion was debated by these same people,— to wit, Resolved, Would crime and poverty exist under a system whereby production and distribution were under control of the people?— I am just as posi-tive the answer would be, No: poverty or crime could not exist. Let this be the subject of debate between our great colleges, and statistics and facts will be brought to light that will astonish the world.

If the people understand these questions and answers, and after mature consideration are convinced of the truth of both conclusions, why should they not make an individual effort to bring about the desired change? It is only by the combined efforts of a large num-ber of individuals that such a great undertaking can be successfully launched. Individuals must have confidence, and back it up with influence and capital, if they wish to inspire confidence in others; for this reform must be carried out by business methods, its line of action being to enter into competition with the present system of production and distribution, and by power of capital and economy, crush it out.

With the disappearance of our present system of struggling for material wealth, selfishness would be unknown, and war would be a barbarism of the past. If the system should first find its foothold in North America, its economic position and justice would force every civilized country on the globe to a like condition, or they would become depopulated. Above all, poverty and crime would disappear, and their attending satellites — ignorance, sickness, and misery — would be known no more; and the latent germs of reason and truth would rise, like Phœnix, from the ruins of decaying superstition.

With all the progress that has been made in science, art, and the invention and development of labor-saving machinery, no advantage has accrued to the laboring classes. They are in a worse position to-day than twenty years ago: more people are out of employment, and poverty is more general; and never in the world's history has crime been so prolific or wide-spread as in the United States to-day. The subject-matter of our daily papers is more than half a record of crime, and thousands of courts are kept busy trying criminal cases. This criminal class is not confined to the lower strata, but has invaded the precincts of education and refinement, and includes many who hold positions of trust in banks, insurance companies, large corporations, and business houses. Bank-wrecking, forgery, defalcation, and many minor crimes are of almost daily occurrence among this class. No man is trusted, honesty is at a discount, and bonds are demanded to insure against dishonesty; and it only needs incentive and opportunity for the average individual to develop into a first-class criminal. Is this not a terrible state of affairs, when honesty has grown so cold and decrepit that bonds are demanded to insure against its downfall? Is there not something radically wrong in a system which breeds dishonesty?

Crime is an effect, the cause of which must be removed before we can hope to rid society of its presence. Punishment for crime is only local in effect, and does not in any sense reach or remove the cause; and laws might be made from now to eternity for the purpose of restricting crime, but as long as competition for material wealth existed, crime would flourish.

In the distorted features of humanity, you can see the results of centuries of competition. Avarice, greed, brutality, cunning, and all the other hideous deformities of the mind are mirrored on the face of man, and depict with unfailing accuracy the mind within. Under the state of equality which would result from the success of the United Company, every individual feature would put on a look of intelligence, genius, and beauty. The distorted features of crime and poverty, with their furrows of anxiety and care, would fade away before the brilliant light of a new-found happiness and freedom. The mind within would spring upward with a bound, when relieved of its load of oppression and the chains of slavery which have bound it down to a life of toil and drudgery. Then, in its free and natural condition, it would expand and blossom into inconceivable beauty and power ; and earth would become a heaven beyond the ideal imagination.

The mind is naturally virtuous, honest, ambitious, and progressive. It is not made of material that turns backward. But, under our present business and social system, it is hemmed in by circumstances over which it has no individual control ; and, there being no unity of action, the result is a chaotic system, which necessitates an endless system of laws. The only remedy is such a change as will recognize the rights of the community as a whole, anterior to the rights of individuals, which would remove the possibility of poverty. Without this change, all the power of the law and all the preaching and charity in the world can make no headway against the constantly increasing tendency to crime. Criminal acts are but symptoms of the diseased condition of our system ; and it is a long road to travel for moralists who wish to eradicate disease, to try to do so by curing symptoms, when the cause itself is continually breeding its pestilential germs.

Book II.

THE HUMAN DRIFT

The Interview:

An Anticipation

THE INTERVIEW.

The following interview taken verbatim from the *Standard*, shortly before this second edition of "The Human Drift" went to press, which gives a general idea of the reception by the public of the proposition to establish a United Company, and the eagerness with which they grasped the opportunity to escape from their present deplorable condition, will be of interest to those of my readers who have not before clearly understood the object in view in forwarding such an enterprise.

Mr. X., the gentleman interviewed, is too well known to need an introduction here. His ability and judgment in the commercial world are unquestioned, and in financial affairs and enterprises of great magnitude he has been the acknowledged leader for many years. His success has been mainly due to his keen insight into the future, which he anticipated by reasoning from cause to effect; and in this last step, his indorsement of the United Company, he has been largely the means of influencing others to likewise invest their money. Thus the golden flood has been diverted from other channels into the Company's treasury.

That Mr. X. should withdraw from every enterprise with which he had been identified for years, and reinvest his capital in the United Company, was sufficient in itself to make the average man of business pause long enough to analyze the causes which could lead to such a step. Although the United Company had assumed proportions that would have assured its success before Mr. X. had identified himself with it, it was not until such time that it began to command the attention of the general public. With Mr. X.'s indorsement, what had been considered the dream of an enthusiast began to take the form of reality, and those who before were un-reasoning sceptics became the most enthusiastic supporters.

[STANDARD, NEW YORK, AUG. 2, 1896.]

REVOLUTION !

THE UNITED COMPANY

Mr. X. gives his Views to the Public

SAYS THE SUCCESS OF THE COMPANY IS ASSURED

That it is only a Question of Time, and a very Short Time at that, when the Present System of

COMPETITION AND CRIME

Will be relegated to an Ignorant Age

Just at this time, when the public are about recovering from their first surprise at the sudden withdrawal of Mr. X. from those numerous large enterprises which might be called the children of his own brain, and whose birth and progress have been largely due to his individuality and perseverance, only to transfer his allegiance to the United Company, which, though known in a general way before, was not thought seriously of by the public until it became known that it had received a sudden influx of eighty million dollars and the support of Mr. X., it may be of interest to many, who stand in fear and trembling of the result, to learn through Mr. X. the future plans of the Company.

Reporter.— Mr. X., you must be aware of the sudden interest of the public in everything connected with the United Company since it has received your indorsement and support, both financially and as an advocate of its power to bring production and distribution to a scientific basis of economy. Are you willing to give, through the medium of the *Standard*, the causes which led you to believe in the United Company?

Mr. X.— I have no objection to giving the public any information in my power, and why I believe in the United Company and know it will meet with success; but, before going further, I should like to say to the public that there is no personality in the United Company, and I do not wish to be singled out more than another. My financial interest for the time being may be greater than others; but, if you have followed the United Company to its future logical conclusion, you must be aware that my personal interest is no more than others. To many it should mean a great deal more, as they will be raised to a material equality with those above them. By this you will understand that it is not the purpose of the United Company to force the educated and wealthy class down to the level of the poor and ignorant, but just the reverse,— to, in fact, raise the poor and ignorant up to a level with his more fortunate brother, and to carry mankind, as a whole, far beyond present material and educational possibilities.

Reporter.—What induced you to give the United Company your support?

Mr. X.— That seems like an easy question to answer, but in a way it is embarrassing; for my investment in this Company was the result of the same analysis and judgment which induced me to make all previous investments,— safety of capital and surety of profit. So you can see the basis sprang from a selfish motive, but I can give a better answer to the question by giving the chain of incidents which led up to my investment. The story will be both interesting and instructive to those who are speculative in a philosophical way, as it shows how the merest chance or the most trifling incident will sometimes change the whole current of our lives. I had been in somewhat failing health, resulting probably from too close application to business, when my physician insisted that I should drop everything for a time and travel and rest, else I might break down entirely. Such advice is more easily given than acted upon, when every minute of time is valuable and necessary in the enterprises in which you are engaged. Until that moment, I had never realized the position of slavery in which I was placed. Here I was, a man rated among his fellows the most fortunate because I had a few dollars more than they, and yet I could not call a single hour my own for pleasure. Even though I should tear myself away from

offices and desks and directors' meetings, my mind would continue
to work, and telegrams and messages would follow me wherever I
went.   But to return to the subject: I was finally compelled to
leave the city, and go on an extended trip; but, try as I would, I
could not find the rest required, and was disposed to be despondent
as to the future, when the whole drift of my mind was turned into
another channel.   My thoughts of railroads, telegraphs, and other
interests were swept away.   What had appeared to me before as
mighty enterprises, sank into insignificance when compared with the
one which had been brought to my attention.

You have often been to the theatre when the raising of the cur-
tain would show a complete change of scene : it was so with me.
I had always looked upon humanity through the spectacles of profit
and loss, and had no idea that the defects of society were defects
of the optic nerve of intelligence.   When the truth was finally impressed upon me, I felt like a man who had always walked in darkness, but who had suddenly found the light.   What had always been
confusion before, became a possible scene of beauty and happiness.
It was a revelation, and it happened in this way.

I was sitting in the lobby of the Grand Pacific Hotel in Chicago,
one evening after dinner, when my attention was attracted to the
conversation of a couple of gentlemen who sat near me.   As they
took no pains to subdue their voices and were apparently indifferent to my proximity, I could not well avoid hearing what was said.
They were discussing the labor question ; and I gathered from what
they said that there was to be a meeting that evening, and one of
them was to deliver an address.   I don't know exactly what induced
me to take the step I did.   Probably something said in the course
of their conversation excited my curiosity; but it matters not now.
When these gentlemen had finished their cigars and rose to depart,
I rose also, and followed them, and after a short walk found myself
at their destination.   Although I had had, in connection with my
work, considerable to do with the laboring class, yet I had never
come in actual contact with them or been near one of their meetings.   In fact, I never had any sympathy with them, and always
looked upon them as an antagonistic force, which must succumb
to superior intelligence and power of wealth.   They were valuable,
the same as power developed by a boiler and engine is valuable,
but not half so tractable.   To me the meeting was a novelty, but
not particularly interesting.   It was as I supposed such a meeting
would be, when composed of such elements.   My friend of the
hotel had spoken, and retired amid cheering and general applause;
and I, feeling tired, was about to leave, when the chairman of the
evening stepped forward, and introduced Mr. Henry Bell.   The
name struck me as familiar; and, when I arrested my steps to
turn and see the gentleman, I recognized a former school-mate, and
became interested at once, not alone because I knew him, but
because he was such a contrast to the former speakers.   He had
developed into what his youth had promised, a scholarly gentleman

and a student. His whole bearing bespoke this. He looked more like a college professor than a labor agitator. He was evidently a stranger to most of those present; for his name did not meet with any response when he was introduced, and I could hear those near me asking each other for information. The first clew to his purpose in being there was given when the chairman, in introducing him, said he would deliver an address for the purpose of gaining their support to a company which had recently been formed in the East, called the United Company. I was dimly conscious of having heard of such a company, but that was all; and what I heard from Mr. Bell was a confused jumble at first, but gradually the thread of his discourse began to unravel the knotty points, but the noise and confusion around me were so great that I found it difficult to follow him. He was evidently not appreciated, and cries of " Thieves!" "Monopolists!" and groans and hisses were almost continuous. But he continued to the end; and, though I had heard only portions of his address, I had caught the basis of his argument, and found no difficulty in filling in the missing parts. In conclusion, he advised them to read a book called " The Human Drift," and afterwards send for the prospectus of the United Company.

The crowd were not in sympathy with the plan proposed. They looked upon the United Company as the final effort of the millionnaires to get the whole business of the country centralized in their hands. In other words, the United Company was the King of Monopolies. Notwithstanding all the hue and cry about me, I almost forgot where I was. My mind had grasped the idea, and was conjuring with pictures and mathematics in a way that brought the whole scheme of the United Company before me like a panorama. When the speaker had finished, I made my way to the street as rapidly as possible, and thence to the hotel. There I obtained at the news-stand a copy of the book spoken of; but my mind had worked so rapidly on the basis of the ideas furnished by Mr. Bell that the book only gave additional side-lights to the mental picture which I had already conjured into existence. I read the book through, and the more I resolved the matter in my mind, the more I became convinced that the United Company would be a success. Now it was right here that my business ability, or selfishness, came into play. If the Company should be a success, the longer I delayed participating in its progress, the harder it would be for me to realize on my property. If I sold out now, before depreciation in property began, I could get full values, and by reinvesting in the United Company, could be sure of six per cent. in the event of its success, which my investment would make almost a certainty.

Mr. Bell's assertion that the Company had twenty million dollars in sight convinced me that the public were looking upon the Company with favor. If I went into the Company, my fortune would be saved : if I stayed out, the destruction of the divided business interests of the country would reduce the profits of the carrying trade to a point that would throw my numerous interests into receivers' hands. With my business experience, I could readily see that the United Company, once organized, would be the aggressor in the game of production and distribution, and would be in a position to force every move of its opponents, and eventually crush them. So I quietly went to work, and obtained all the information possible about the Company,— who its promoters were, and what its programme was in inaugurating its business.

Having satisfied myself on these points, I disposed of all my interest in other corporations, and reinvested in this.

Reporter.— When does the United Company expect to begin operations?

Mr. X.— The United Company has already begun operations, inasmuch as its certificate of organization has been filed at Albany, its capital being two hundred and fifty million dollars, which will be increased as occasion may require.

Reporter.— What field will the United Company first enter?

Mr. X.— The first field of production which we shall enter will be the grocery trade; and we will carry everything that is now carried by that trade, except perishable goods. We will establish our manufacturing plant not far from Niagara Falls, and take advantage of that natural power.

Reporter.— What are the principal economies in favor of the United Company?

Mr. X.— They are manifest; and the question would hardly require elucidation with any business man. We have in the United States ten thousand cities and towns, and upward of one million retail stores and twenty-five thousand wholesale stores, which gives a store frontage, averaging them at twenty-five feet, of five thousand miles. This seems incredible, does it not, when you consider that the United Company proposes to reach one-third of our total population within a year, with one hundred stores and no wholesale stores, without saying anything about the thousands of manufacturing establishments it will be the means of closing? The fact is, under our present system it costs more to distribute goods than to produce them.

Of course, it is understood that the objective point of the United Company is a central city, and these one hundred stores will be only temporary, while the process of consolidation is going forward. The manufacture of clothing, shoes, and wearing apparel generally, will follow closely on the manufacture and distribution of groceries. In fact, the United Company expects to cover this whole field inside of five years. It seems like an immense task to accomplish this; but it is only a matter of money, and there is no question on that score. The Company can increase its capital as fast as it can use it.

Before I go any further into the business prospects of the United Company, allow me to hold up before your view a picture that will give you an idea of the great central city in miniature. You probably went to the great World's Fair at Chicago? Yes, well, if you took the necessary time, and were observing, you saw there, gathered together, the machines necessary for forwarding almost every necessary manufacturing industry in the world. In other words, you saw a miniature manufacturing plant capable of producing almost every manufactured product that humanity needs. With this plant, all that the most fastidious taste could desire could be produced. Now, what does this miniature manufacturing world, which combines the greatest skill and inventive genius of mankind, foreshadow? It foreshadows the possibility of a future great "Metropolis," where these machines, multiplied to the necessary requirements to supply the wants of our whole population, are each brought together in its own vast manufacturing establishment at one central point contingent to the great centre of population. In fact, the great exposition at Chicago, especially that part devoted to manufacturing and liberal arts, is an embryo illustration of the future great manufacturing centre of North America,—a perpetual World's Fair, and educator of the people; each separate machine but an integral part of the whole vast industrial machine of the people. The idea is grand, almost overwhelming in its possibilities; and the reality will be the triumph of civilization.

Reporter.— What inducements are offered to subscribers to the stock of the United Company?

Mr. X.— Those who have read the prospectus of the United Company are aware of the terms on which its capital is secured. To induce subscriptions to the first one hundred million of stock, six per cent. was guaranteed for twenty years. Of this I secured seventy million, thirty million having already been subscribed for. I then secured ten million of the second one hundred million, which guarantees a dividend of five per cent. for twenty years. Since my subscription, the balance of the second one hundred million has been taken, and upward of fifty million of the third hundred, which guarantees four per cent. for twenty years. After the third one hundred million has been taken. all future subscriptions will be secured on a guaranteed dividend of three per cent. for twenty years. Beyond these dividends, the stockholders receive no profits whatever, and the cost of product to the consumer will be on a basis of cost of production and distribution, including the interest paid for use of capital.

Reporter.— How will the Company provide for those outside the stockholders and employees, who will be virtually the only ones who will draw any income?

Mr. X.— That is the most serious question which the people have to contend with, and the one which requires the most consideration; for it can be readily understood that production and distribution, as contemplated by the United Company, will not require one-tenth part of the labor now employed for that purpose. The consequence will be just that addition to those already unemployed. To meet this difficulty, it will be necessary that either the government or the United Company shall forward the building of a central city. The United Company will have already begun the work of centralization by establishing the manufacturing interests at one centre. In the building of this wonderful city, all surplus labor can be employed; and it is estimated that there will be accommodation for not less than thirty million people in five years. The undertaking seems stupendous; but it is all a matter of calculation,— a sum in arithmetic which can be easily worked out by any school-boy. If we can erect a certain building in a given time, by a given number of men, it is simply a matter of multiplication to make a thousand, ten thousand, or as many buildings as there are men to employ.

Reporter.— It is believed by many that the United Company will not receive the support from the people that it anticipates; that the people will refuse to purchase goods from the Company, when they realize that every such purchase will weaken their strength as individual competitors.

Mr. X.— People will gravitate to that market where they get the best goods for the least money. It is a natural law which no power on earth can prevent. The United Company will have every advantage in its favor. They will have goods guaranteed pure and unadulterated, and as represented, and at a price that will defy competition. These considerations alone will be fatal to the continued sale of goods the quality and purity of which are a matter of doubt.

Reporter.— Will the United Company, in any instance, compensate those whose business it may destroy?

Mr. X.— No, the United Company enters the lists of competition with the same right as an individual. Individuals do not compensate those whom they destroy by competition. Why should the United Company?

Reporter.— What guarantee have the people that the United Company will not become a monopoly, and absorb the wealth of the country, to the detriment of those who are not stockholders?

Mr. X.— The Company is organized on a basis that makes such a contingency impossible: it is not a private corporation, but is dedicated to the people. Its capital is practically only borrowed, for which it pays a low rate of interest; and no dividends will be paid beyond this interest. This interest is a tax for a limited time only, and was necessary to induce capital to back the enterprise. At the end of twenty years, the Company has the privilege of returning its borrowed capital, and substituting other capital borrowed at the lowest rate of interest possible. But long before that time arrives, the United Company hopes to place production and distribution absolutely in the hands of the people, and dispense with the use of money, or an exchange medium, entirely.

Reporter.— In the grocery trade, will not the people purchase where they can find a variety of every article to choose from?

Mr. X.— I am glad you ask that question; for I hope my answer may explain away a great deal of misconception on the question of variety, and the value of competition between individuals. In the first place, there are not more than fifty distinct manufactured articles in the grocery trade. That is, if you count spices as one, which are produced by one manufacturing establishment; soap as another item; extracts as another, etc.

Under our present system, these fifty items are divided into thousands of establishments; and the goods produced are endless in variety, without any guarantee of purity or standard quality. Now, the question is this: Are the people benefited by this division of business and great variety? We have Babbitt's, Syddall's, Brown's, Dreydopple's, Kirk's, Proctor & Gamble's, and other makes of soap too numerous to mention. Some people like one make, and some another, their preference being largely influenced by advertising, which may have attracted their attention; for the question of advertising cuts the principal figure in placing any goods on the market no matter what their quality may be. This being true, are the public not in a position to be deceived in any goods they purchase, when an advertiser is only limited in his lies by his conscience? Is there any means whereby the people can be absolutely certain of the purity of manufactured articles of consumption?

Now, can any reason be given why the United Company should not make as good or better soaps than any now made? They will be in a position to hire the very best talent that is now employed, and they can use the highest grade of raw materials. They have nothing to gain in making poor goods, for the Company is not a money-making concern. Under these circumstances, would the people continue to purchase soaps of which they had no guarantee of purity, or would they purchase of the United Company, where they had positive knowledge of its purity? The Company will manufacture sufficient variety to meet the different uses for which soap is required. The same is true of spices, baking powder, and, in fact, every article of the grocery trade; and the Company would have as many items as are now carried, but not the variety of brands, which is unnecessary. In every instance, their goods will be the best that highest grade of material and science can produce; and the public will be certain that they are as represented.

Reporter.— How will the business of the United Company be conducted?

Mr. X.— Strictly on a cash basis, both in buying and selling. Not a single credit account will be opened. No insurance will be carried, and we will do our own banking. All raw material will be purchased from first hands, only to leave the Company's possession when purchased by the consumer.

Reporter.— Is not the organization of the United Company in opposition to the rights of the people?

Mr. X.— The United Company is not in opposition to existing laws, though its purpose is to destroy that worn-out theory that competition is the life of trade. It only anticipates, by years, what must be the result of the present tendency to consolidate business, which is a natural law of attraction to greater economy in production. The United Company is only doing what one private individual might do if he had sufficient capital; and individual fortunes are rapidly reaching that mark where they could enter almost any line of trade, and control it.   When it comes to individual corporations, they are springing into existence every day, and gradually consolidating and absorbing different branches of business.   The only difference between these corporations and the United Company, is that the individual corporations are in for making all that they can out of the people, and the stockholders get rich at their expense; while the United Company is organized in the interest of the people.   It would be a strange condition of affairs if any representative of the people at Washington, should give voice in opposition to the right of the people to organize for the purpose of producing and distributing the necessities of life more economically.

Reporter.— What interests will be first affected when the Company commences operations ?

Mr. X.— All interests will be more or less affected from the start, for it can be readily understood that whatever the United Company secures must necessarily be drawn from the divided interests of the country ; and, from cause to effect, it will not only affect those trades whose goods they manufacture and sell, but it will affect the whole contributary and tributary system to those trades.   But the interest which will be soonest affected and suffer the most rapid and disastrous depreciation will be real estate values in our cities, which already, in anticipation of the inevitable, are in a panicky condition. When we consider that real estate has always been looked upon as the most secure form of investment, it is marvellous to find that it is the first to be affected by this revolution.

Reporter.— What are the Company's plans as regards New York City ?

Mr. X.— The United Company will enter New York City with the prospect of doing a retail trade direct with the people, of not less than one hundred million dollars per year, and it does not take much calculation to find that this must put the shutters up to thousands of wholesale and retail stores, factories, etc.   That which has held the city together and made it what it is, is no longer present.   The population must look elsewhere for employment.   Following closely the absorption of divided interests, such as groceries, clothing, shoes, etc., will come the downfall of all those interests which depended on their divided continuance, such as law, banking, insurance, stock speculation, and brokerage and commission   In fact, the whole system will be destroyed ; and hundreds of branches of business will disappear entirely.

Reporter.— How many stockholders are there now in the Company, and how do the subscriptions run ?

Mr. X.— Here is a copy as taken from the books as they stand to-day.   It gives the number of subscribers and amounts from three thousand dollars and upwards, and the number of subscribers to various amounts below three thousand dollars, of which number more than twenty thousand subscribed below one hundred dollars, and more than eight thousand of these subscribed for only one share of stock, costing one dollar. The total number of subscribers and amount of stock in aggregate that has been issued is given at foot of columns : —

Subscribers.	Amount.	Total.
1	$80,000,000	$80,000,000
1	12,000,000	12,000,000
3	3,000,000	15,000,000
9	2,000,000	18,000,000
16	1,000,000	16,000,000
1	750,000	750,000
22	500,000	11,000,000
35	200,000	7,000,000
67	100,000	6,700,000
1	60,000	60,000
74	50,000	3,750,000
5	40,000	200,000
3	30,000	90,000
163	25,000	4,075,000
82	20,000	1,640,000
4	18,000	72,000
2	16,000	32,000
120	12,000	1,440,000
275	10,000	2,750,000
14	9,000	120,000
88	8,000	704,000
168	7,000	1,176,000
449	6,000	2,694,000
4,892	5,000	24,460,000
3,477	4,000	13,908,000
3,127	3,500	10,944,500
3,963	3,000	11,889,000
37,621 in amounts under	3,000	22,732,463
Total, 57,683		Total, $269,186,963

Reporter.— How will labor, capital, and our political parties be effected by the success of the United Company?

Mr. X.—When the workingman understands the objective point of the United Company, he will co-operate with others to make it a success. The wealthy individuals of to-day have a different class to deal with than has been known in past history. " A little knowledge is a dangerous thing "; and the laboring classes have just sufficient knowledge at present to know that they are the actual producers of wealth, and yet practically slaves. This knowledge makes them dangerous, and a constant menace to existing institutions. They know they are oppressed, but their knowledge is not sufficient to give them a solution to the problem. The result is a resort to brute methods, and at the present time, the outlook is rapidly assuming the possibility of civil war against capital. Never, in the history of man, has there been the intelligence displayed by the working classes that has been shown within the last few years in their wide-spread organization to combat the tendency of capital to force them to a lower position of slavery.

This has resulted on the part of the workingmen in strikes and demands that have met with but partial success; but, as the organizations increase, amalgamate, and grow stronger both in number and financially, they will become a power that will compel recognition. It has already been necessary to call out government and State militia in several of the States to quell disturbances resulting from these strikes; and, *when it becomes necessary to conduct business at the bayonet point, it does not require much argument to prove the system itself wrong.*

It would require many times the available force of arms in the United States to protect property and non-union workers, should a general strike on the railroads of the country ever become a possibility. One such strike would paralyze the whole productive and distributive interests of the States; and, if maintained for a month, the suffering in our large cities and towns from lack of food supplies would be beyond knowledge. That such a strike is in the minds of the railroad employees, and is set down for the near future, I firmly believe; and to maintain the present system under such circumstances, will necessitate an army greater than that of either Germany or France. Laboring men cannot be blamed for organizing, and they cannot be blamed for striking. Under our system of *might makes right*, legislation, the making of laws, is wholly in the hands of capital; and the only recourse labor has to offset this power which hedges them in and holds them down, is to strike. If they win, they are in the right: if they lose, they are in the wrong; for success in warfare gives right to the victor. This brute principle of progress must continue to be recognized until such time when new light will dawn on the masses, and they will demand and secure material equality. If the capitalists and the laboring men would look closely into the face of this labor problem, they would see that the strained relations between them must continue to a climax. Their interests are not mutual, but opposed to each other at every point. Knowing this, and seeing what the inevitable result must be if they continue to drift apart, it should be the interest of both to establish production and distribution on a more rational basis.

The intelligent citizen should be guided by principles founded upon his own judgment, not by political fanaticism. The Republican and Democratic parties have both failed in their attempt to better the condition of the people; and no government has within it the vital spark of continuity that is only held together by an intricate system of arbitrary laws. And the only government which can dispense with such laws is one where mutual responsibility and interest in production and distribution are the foundation of material prosperity. When such a condition is attained, and the labor of production and distribution falls with equal justice on each individual of a community, *then, and not till then, can we say that we have a government which has within it the vital spark of life.*

There is cohesion, strength, and economy, in union. But under a system of competition, where the individual interests are divided, and each is struggling for mastery, it must necessarily follow that there would be waste and extravagance, and lack of cohesion of individuals to fixed principles. The wider the division of particles under the system of competition, the greater the proportion of waste for a given amount of production.

Reporter.— Does not the contemplated abandonment of our thousands of cities and towns, which have demanded the labor of upwards of a hundred years to bring to their present advanced condition, involve the question of fearful loss of accumulated wealth?

Mr. X.— Apparently, yes; in reality, no. It is a well-known fact that the progressive manufacturer does not hesitate to abandon an old machine for one of more modern construction that will save manual labor. He knows that the question of saving labor will soon make up for the loss in the abandonment of the old machine and the cost of the new one. On this same principle, I look upon our thousands of cities and towns, with their millions of stores, manufacturing establishments, and houses, and our scattered farming interests, and transportation system of wagons, horses, and railroads, with all their intricate parts, simply as a vast machine of production and distribution,— only a means to an end. Now, if we, with our modern ideas, can construct a machine which will involve less labor and power in arriving at that end, we are justified in abandoning the old machine for the new.

The present machine is so intricate that it is beyond comprehension. It involves so many ramifications and intricate parts that it is constantly getting out of repair, and our legislators are in a constant tempest of excitement in trying to keep the unwieldy monster from flying the track altogether. The Republicans open the throttle wide, while the Democrats are straining every nerve to down brakes. Thus the public find themselves between contending forces, either of which is liable at any time to crush the very life out of the republic.

There would be none of this contention when the new machine had taken the place of the old. There would be no contending forces, no parties, no politics, but a united and homogeneous intelligence, with one object in view,— the continual improvement of products and the machine of production.

Reporter.— On what basis of calculation do you specify the time limit of ten years, when production and distribution will be in the hands of the people?

Mr. X.— On the basis of the United Company's power to cover the whole field of necessary production in that time, except, possibly, the farming interests. With unlimited capital, we can enter every field at almost the same time; and, if it is possible to control one branch of production, it is just as possible to control all, and proportionately more economical.

Reporter.— How can the people ever hope to adjust themselves to such a sudden revolution?

Mr. X.— Under these conditions, there would be no reduction in the amount of necessary products, such as food and clothing, and means would be found whereby they would find their way to necessary channels; and, as I before remarked, the projecting and building of "Metropolis" would require every available hand and brain. Manufacturing establishments to this end, that would astonish the world in their magnitude, would spring into existence, such as iron mills, where possibly hundreds of thousands of men would be employed. And just as rapidly as men were thrown out of employment under the old system, they would find employment under the new. It is a wonderful subject to contemplate; and, the more it is thought of, the more perfect becomes the picture of the future. It is only a question of capital and a fair start, and no power in the world can retard its consummation. To live through this evolution of excitement and change, would be to secure a period of happiness that has never been vouchsafed to man in the past, and probably would never be equalled in the future.

Reporter.— Do you believe the time will come when an exchange medium will be dispensed with?

Mr. X.— Yes, in twenty-five years at the latest, and probably in considerably less time. Under a system of material equality, an exchange medium would be wholly impracticable, and involve a useless amount of labor in establishing values of products based on the labor involved in their production; and, what is more to the point, it would leave an opening for crime. On the other hand, by making all the products of toil free, the last vestige of reason for crime disappears.

The general average of consumption would be about the same, though individual tastes might widely differ. It is my belief that the people, under conditions of material equality, would be rational in all their desires, more so than under existing conditions. They would no longer have an incentive to accumulate; and those traits of character which spring from selfishness and vanity, which have their birth under our system of competition, would disappear.

Reporter.— Would foreigners, as emigrants, be admitted to the country to participate in our material welfare?

Mr. X.— Yes, upon the payment of the stipulated requirement of labor. This is the fundamental principle of justice. Each individual must pay, by labor, for the material benefits which are the result of labor. There is no escape for any one in this regard. Every one must put his shoulder to the wheel of necessity, and add his just payment to its propulsion.

Reporter.— What will be the effect of the success of the United Company on foreign governments?

Mr. X.— It is hard to say; but such success would probably mean the rapid disintegration of all governments, for the people would have their eyes opened to the defects of those governments.

Reporter.— What will be the effect on our exports and imports?

Mr. X.— Our whole system of exchange with foreign countries will undergo a change. We will only produce an excess of goods beyond our needs to an amount sufficient to answer purpose of exchange for such foreign products as we do not produce. Thus we can exchange wheat, corn, cotton, etc., for teas, coffees, spices, etc.

We shall not import any foods or clothing which it is possible for us to produce ourselves.

Reporter.— Is there any other information which you think would be of interest to the public?

Mr. X.— Any one who is enthusiastic on this subject, and understands the possibilities of the future, might talk indefinitely; but enough has been said to give a general idea of the plans of the United Company. I can only say, in conclusion, that the Company offers opportunities for the future happiness of the whole people such as the world has never known.

[EDITORIAL, STANDARD, AUG. 2, 1896.]

THE UNITED COMPANY.

That the commercial field is the proper channel of reform, will be generally conceded; but that humanity can adjust itself to the rapid evolutionary changes that must result if the United Company is allowed to enter the field of competition, is a question of most grave apprehension, and should at once demand the attention of our State legislators and national government.

Though this reform movement, founded as it is on economic business methods, has a basis of logic that admits of but one conclusion, and that conclusion one which should be the ardent desire of every humanitarian, still we should not allow excitement and enthusiasm to carry us beyond the bounds of reason or blind us to the inevitable effects that must follow in the wake of such a revolution. This revolution has been most fitly compared by the author of "The Human Drift" to an earthquake which destroys cities and towns in a single night. Now, we are not prepared to adjust ourselves to an earthquake of this description. If the conclusion of this reform movement would result in the perfect civilization described, cannot this end be attained without these intervening years of disturbance? Cannot a United Party enter the political field with the idea in view of forwarding the building of "Metropolis," under government supervision, and gradually centring the people in that city, to be employed on its further extension, and eventually gradually absorb the industrial field?

We stand face to face with the problem, and it must be worked out without unnecessary delay. Either we must allow the United Company to continue without legislative obstruction, or the government, otherwise the people, must at once devise a plan that will satisfy the clamor for reform. The pathway to a perfect civilization has been pointed out, and the people demand the right of way.

THE HUMAN DRIFT

SUPPLEMENT.

In the preceding interview, and in the editorial comments on the same, two questions have been brought forward,— How will humanity adjust itself to the rapid changes resulting from the progress of the United Company, and how will the increasing numbers who are thrown out of employment find the means whereby the necessities of life may be obtained? That these questions are of grave and serious moment, I will admit, but that they should be considered in the light of positive objections, in view of the object which the United Company seeks to attain, no sane man or woman will believe. Humanity always has adjusted itself to changed conditions of environment, and in the present evolution it will do the same.

Already, in anticipation of the contraction of the field of labor by the action of the United Company, and the belief that the United Company is destined to attract the people to a central city, a United People's Party has sprung into existence, with the avowed purpose of getting control of the government and forwarding the building of " Metropolis." Its purposes are not antagonistic to the interests of the United Company, but a great aid, as it lifts from the shoulders of the United Company the burden of responsibility for those thrown out of employment, and leaves the United Company free to rapidly absorb and centralize production and distribution. It will be noticed by the certificate published here, which sets forth the articles of faith and platform of the United People's Party, that they confine themselves, as a party, within very narrow limits. It is not a platform setting forth their purpose of mending and patching the present machinery of production and distribution, but a revolutionary document, that contemplates nothing less than the total destruction of the present system, and in its place the establishment of material equality. The platform is one upon which our whole people should stand ; and the United People's Party is prepared to supply every labor organization and political club with any number of these certificates, to be signed and returned to the Central Bureau of the United People's Party at Boston. and at the present time they are being signed and returned by thousands from every State

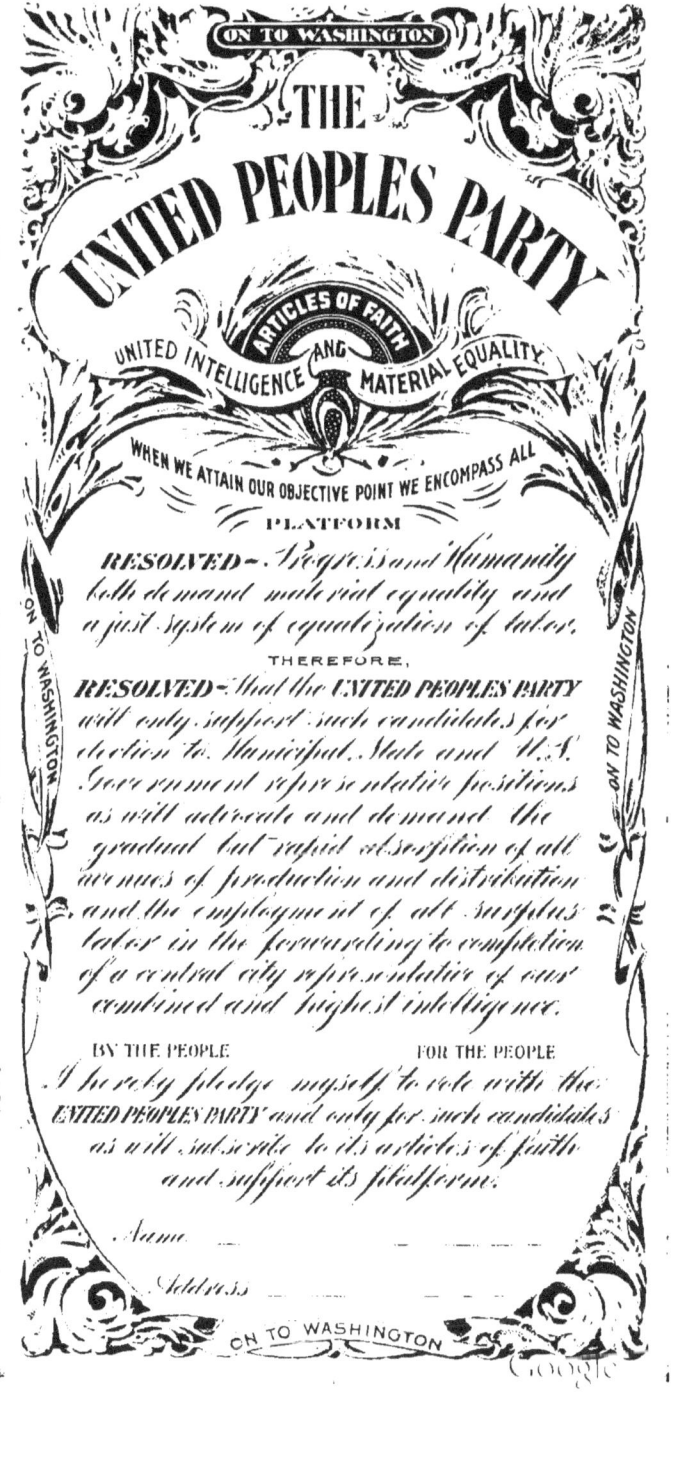

ON TO WASHINGTON

THE UNITED PEOPLES PARTY

ARTICLES OF FAITH

UNITED INTELLIGENCE AND MATERIAL EQUALITY.

WHEN WE ATTAIN OUR OBJECTIVE POINT WE ENCOMPASS ALL

PLATFORM

RESOLVED – Progress and Humanity both demand material equality and a just system of equalization of labor.

THEREFORE,

RESOLVED – That the UNITED PEOPLES PARTY will only support such candidates for election to Municipal, State and U.S. Government representative positions as will advocate and demand the gradual but rapid absorption of all avenues of production and distribution and the employment of all surplus labor in the forwarding to completion of a central city representative of our combined and highest intelligence.

BY THE PEOPLE   FOR THE PEOPLE

I hereby pledge myself to vote with the UNITED PEOPLES PARTY and only for such candidates as will subscribe to its articles of faith and support its platform.

Name

Address

in the Union, and the next few years will see many of the party's representatives returned to Senate and House. There will be no misunderstanding of these representatives' purposes in being there. Their platform is sound, and easy to comprehend. Republicanism and Democracy, the illegitimate children of Monarchy, are no better than the parent who gave them birth. The same misery, poverty, and crime surround us. Liberty is only a name : it is not a reality. *Material equality must be established.*

The people can and will rise to the occasion, and dissipate the fear of the masses ; and nothing can better illustrate the resources of the government in times of emergency than to call the attention of the public to the War of the Rebellion. This was one of the greatest disasters the civilized world has ever known, and a crime that will always remain a blot upon the civilization of the nineteenth century. Though the object to be attained was worthy of the greatest effort, still the means employed was a crime. Is the combined intelligence of the people so low that a court of nations could not arbitrate and settle every national or international dispute ? Why should the law interfere with individuals in their manner of settling by force matters of dispute, when nations of individuals, with their combined intelligence, are unable to settle the most trivial national or international difficulties without resorting to the barbarous custom of war ? Does might make right ? Does victory always perch upon the banner of justice ? If I am called a liar, and in return knock my traducer down, he can have me arrested, and the probability is I would be fined or sent to prison ; and yet a nation which says I must not uphold my own dignity or resent an insult, but must present my grievances to a court of law, will, for less sufficient cause, considering the gravity of war with its train of untold misery and uncertainty, resort to that most barbarous practice, strength of arms in the adjustment of difficulties ; and to this end, every nation on the globe keeps its standing army and navy in readiness for revenge, murder, and rapine. What else can we conclude from this than that the individual mind is but a reflection of our national policy ? Why should we condemn the action of the individual, when a nation itself is a rowdy, and always ready to resort to physical power at the least provocation.

But my indignation carries me away from the subject. My purpose in this article is only to show the ability of the people to meet the present crisis in the contraction of the field of labor. To do this, it is only necessary to present for your contemplation two pictures : first, a picture of the Civil War of thirty odd years ago, which divided a common government into two opposing armies, which destroyed thousands of lives, ruined millions of dollars' worth of property, and cost upward of $2,700,000,000 to the North alone.

During this war, when our population was less than half what it is now, millions of men came to the front, and were ready to lay down their lives in what they considered humanity's cause. Men left their business and comfortable homes, and tore themselves from sweethearts, wives, children, and all that they held most dear, to accept the desperate chances of war and all the discomforts and privations of a soldier's life. Of the number who went away, upward of 67,000 were killed on the field of battle, upward of 40,000 died from their wounds, 200,000 died from disease, and more than 40,000 died from other causes. The total of the Union forces who were killed and died was upward of 349,000. The total number that formed the army of the Union was upward of 2,770,000, which in time served, reduced to an average of three years, gave 2,326,000 for a period of that time. The number of Union men captured and imprisoned during the war was upward of 212,000.

When we contemplate the number who never returned to their homes, having been either killed on the battlefield or succumbed to that more horrible fate,— slow death in the poisoned atmosphere of prisons and hospitals,— and the many shattered in health from privation and exposure, maimed and crippled for life, who returned to drag out a miserable existence, is it not strange that some more rational means of freeing the slaves was not considered possible?

If men can be raised to such enthusiasm that they will deliberately face a shower of leaden hail, and invite death in other and more hideous forms in the defence of an alien part of humanity, what can we expect if in this much greater and more far-reaching cause in the interest of *all* humanity, this same enthusiasm should spring into life? It would result in such a revolution as the world has never witnessed. Death, destruction, pillage, and misery would not follow in its wake. Wives would not be made widows, children would not be made fatherless, but life, light, and reason would be born in the heart of every individual, and there would rise to the skies such a city and such a civilization as the world has never known or dreamed of as possible.

If we could feed, clothe, and arm nearly three millions of men, and keep them in the field for a period of three years in their work of destruction, murder, and pillage, and foot the bill to the amount of nearly three billion dollars, and afterwards pay in pensions nearly two billions more (which will probably amount to as much again before the last pensioner is gone), without saying anything about the loss in commercial affairs resulting from the strife, and the loss to progress of the labor and intelligence of those who enlisted, and without saying anything of the losses of the South, and the misery that follows in the wake of all war,— I say, if we can do all this and stand it without complaint, would it not be possible now, when the country has double the population, for us to put in the field, and feed, clothe, and arm with weapons of industry, an army of five million men for the purpose of building the great city "Metropolis"?

The first army was sent on a mission of destruction, and every dollar that it cost was lost. This second army would be sent on its mission of intelligent labor. It would cost no more to maintain this army of *construction* than it did to maintain the army of *destruction;* but what would be the result in five years,— a period equal to the time the war lasted? We would have that to show for our money which would make the whole world look on with envy and wonder. We would have a city well under way which would make London, Paris, Berlin, Vienna, and New York look like the work of ignorant savages in comparison. Five years would see ten millions of our population sleeping within its environment; ten years, thirty millions; and in less than twenty-five years, or before 1920, the city would be complete in all its essential parts. At that time, its population would not be less than ninety million souls.

They who laugh and decry the possibility of such a change in so short a time, do so without thinking. They do not realize the wonderful power that would result from the concentration of the energy of millions of men and women who had a common focus in view. There is no focus to present endeavor; but once let humanity grasp the idea of a great central city, and a future of material equality, and every mind would be focussed on one spot, and have one determined end in view. The city would actually spring into existence, as far as individual comprehension could see ; for its rapid growth would be beyond the mind to follow in detail.

Let us step aside from the well-beaten track of ages, which is only one long hideous record of crime and misery, and boldly follow the light of our combined and highest intelligence. Let us do something that will make life worth living, and at the same time, escape this monotonous grind that only results in worry, anxiety, and misery. We have found Aladdin's lamp. Let us profit by its possession.

Book III.

THE HUMAN DRIFT

The Consummation:
A New Civilization

It is the duty of every father and mother to guide the footsteps of their children, and to distribute their love and favor equally among them. And on this same just principle, the government, which stands in the relation of parent to its numerous subjects, should distribute equally its love and favor among those who are dependent on its protection.

SATAN'S LAMENT.*

Millions of years have come and gone
Since I was hurled, an unclean thing,
Into the fathomless depths of space,
From out the gates of Eternal Spring.
And now again I hear the sound
Of weeping angels, as they cry:
Repent! It never is too late
Till after you have cast the die.
My power was broken; my reign was o'er.
Repent I would not: what was more
I would not for my life implore.
So, going forth from those gates of light,
I leaped into the darkest night,
And landed here upon the earth
Just as the germ of life had birth.
Once more I placed my pickets round,
Of selfish power; and bound them down
With bands of avarice and greed,
To let them on each other feed.
And now, again enthroned in state,
With power supreme o'er human fate,
I spread my nets of sin and crime
From pole to pole, through every clime,
To catch the souls that tripped and fell,
And made the earth a living hell.
The heart of man I turned to stone,
And tears of pity gave him none,
Except for self; and filled his brain
With passion's lust for wealth and fame,—
Not fame that comes from solid worth,

---

* Satan is here represented as selfishness, a power which dominates and directs the unreasoning intelligence, which is finally driven forth by the birth of Reason.

That raises men above the earth,
But fame that has its roots in mire,
That reeks with crime, and mad desire
To hold within his single mind
The fate of millions of his kind.
The God of man I made of gold;
Material wealth, to win and hold;
And its possession made the price
Of happiness throughout their life.
Then, like a pack of wolves at bay,
They fought like demons night and day;
And through the gates of hell they trod,
To gain possession of their God.
And I looked on this dance of death,
This reigning power of selfishness,
With fiendish joy; for I knew well
It kept alight the fires of hell.
Through all these years they battle wage,
Like beasts of prey shut in a cage; .
While on my throne, in ghoulish glee,
I watch their struggles to be free.
But bars were strong, and locked the gate,
And life hung by the thread of fate;
And those who tried to 'scape their doom
Found only rest beyond the tomb.
No sleep was theirs: each soul was placed
Against all others of his race.
The price of bread was strength to stand
Against the world, a single hand.
The mind was made to think of heaven,
A life beyond the one here given.
The charm it worked: the rising mist
Shut out the hope of earthly bliss.
Then hope, eternal in the breast,
Raised temples to that future rest
Beyond the rounded vault of blue;
And peace on earth was lost to view.
My work was done: within my grasp
I held their souls, from first to last;
And every one was steeped in crime,
And in the mesh of hell confined.

And then, like men who rise to power,
I felt secure, up to the hour
When, waking from a troubled dream,
The light of Reason round me streamed.
And now the sentence of my crime
Comes back through all those years of time.
" Your sin is selfishness and greed,
And power o'er souls on which to feed.
Go forth unto the realm of space,
The King of Terror to every race,—
From orb to orb to take your flight,
And do your deeds at dead of night.
In sleep your eyes may never close,
Your brain must never take repose.
For, should the light of Reason dawn,
Your power o'er souls is surely gone ;
And they will cast you into space,
To find another resting-place."
So, ever since that fatal day,
My restless soul, in black array,
Has travelled forth, and in the gloom
Of night has cast its nets of doom
O'er souls of men, and, like a spell,
Made every orb of light a hell.
But woe is mine : the round of years
Brings to my eyes those bitter tears
Which come to all who rise to fame
And selfish power by crime and shame,
Who, heeding not the voice within,
Trample the souls of men in sin,
And, looking down from their throne of state,
Calmly gaze on the wrecks of fate,
And watch the tears of sorrow flow,
An endless flood of endless woe,
And caring not that in their breast
They nurse the crime of selfishness.
'Tis so with me. The morning light
Shows that my soul is black as night.
I would repent, but now too late.
Once more I've cast the die of fate,
Which says you cannot backward tread,

And by repentance save the dead.
And now again I, waking, find
Security is but a blind
That wooes to sleep, and in that sleep
Steals the power that you would keep.
The darkest hour of crime and sin
The world had ever known or been
Was just before I went to rest
Upon my bed of selfishness ;
And who'd have thought, in all that strife,
The reasoning germ would spring to life,
And from the darkest hour of night
Would spring the dawn of coming light,
Which shows the gate of hope confined
Within the blackness of the mind?
Ignorance, o'er which my power
Has reigned supreme up to this hour,
Has passed away, and in its place
The head of Reason shows its face.
What's that I see on yonder plain !
The walls of hell are rent in twain ;
And, streaming out from every side,
The souls of men are seen to glide.
I must away ! My time has come.
Crime has lost, and virtue won;
And now farewell. No longer we
On the same planet can agree.
So, under cover of the night,
To yonder orb I'll take my flight;
And there, before the break of day,
Or Reason's dawn, I'll have full sway.
And over all I'll cast the spell
Of Satan's power to make a hell.

EPILOGUE.

No one can read the lines of fate
Beyond the bar of Reason's gate.
The past is but a shaded line,—
The progress of the human mind
From outer darkness unto light,

Along whose rays we wing our flight.
And, as we near approach the door
From which the light is seen to pour,
The square of distance from the goal
Sheds greater light upon the soul.
But none the future path can trace,
Or leap across the depths of space,
Or tell from whence that light does come,—
The great eternal central sun ;
But, step by step, must win his way
Through endless time, Eternity.

THE NEW CIVILIZATION.

INTRODUCTION.

Material equality must result in a new civilization, new in every part of its structure of mind and matter. The whole aspect of nature must assume new meanings and ends, for they will be seen by new senses of interpretation. With our present individual knowledge, we cannot conceive it; or, if we could conceive it, we would not believe it possible.

It was not my intention when the subject-matter of "The Human Drift" was outlined, to supplement it with a description of what civilization might be when production and distribution had been resolved to the point of greatest economy; but, if the mind once gets thoroughly interested in the subject of consolidation and centralization, it cannot escape the logical conclusion,— *a perfect civilization.*

In my description of this new civilization, I do not leap into the future and make scientific discoveries which are not discovered yet, neither do I anticipate wonderful inventions which are not invented yet, nor do I annihilate time and anticipate the future of art. I confine myself to our present progressive position, and only utilize that which we now have of art, science, and invention in its most economical application.

I look upon the consolidation of business and its centralization from a purely business standpoint. I see enormous business enterprises that demand millions of dollars running as smoothly as though they were controlled by a single individual mind. Yet the controlling power of these large corporations is the combined intelligence of a large number of individuals. Under these circumstances, the corporation has within it the elements of continuous life; for the death of any single or number of individuals would not disturb its progress. This same idea would be also true of a civilization that was combined as one intelligence. It would have the elements of continuous life, and nothing could disturb its continuous progress.

Can any one with an artistic mind see beauty in our present cities and towns, which are built haphazard, without any idea of uniformity in structure and design,— tall and short buildings, brick, wood, stone, and iron buildings, old and new buildings, palaces, tenements, and factories, breweries, stables, and saloons, thrown together along our narrow and ill-paved thoroughfares, as though they had been dropped from the clouds without any idea of arrangement? Crime, poverty, filth, and degradation are found next door to opulence and voluptuous extravagance. Here is a building which apparently combines every modern improvement in our knowledge of art, science, and invention; while within a stone's throw are others that would disgrace the dark ages.

Can it be said that our cities combine our highest intelligence in plan and construction? Would it not be reasonable to suppose, that in building a city which was to combine within its environment a population of thousands or millions of people, the people as a whole should build that city, and thus combine its intelligence to make that city a symmetrical and beautiful artistic conception?

Under our system of competition, we have the very rich and the very poor, with all the intervening gradations of society. This results in a companion picture in the architecture of our cities, for we find the palace and the filthy hovel and all the intervening gradations of habitations.

Under a system of material equality, each individual would be on a par in his material possessions, each individual would be on a par in advantage of education, *and the city would reflect their combined intelligence in its perfect construction.*

After hundreds of years of opportunity, we still find ourselves surrounded by an ignorant and a filthy environment. We are obliged to breathe the contaminated atmosphere of crime and misery, and to rub shoulder to shoulder with brutes in human form. Who is to blame? Who but ourselves; for we have the power to change all this, and surround ourselves with an environment of virtue and happiness.

Before I begin a description of my conception of this new civilization possible in the immediate future, I would like to ask each of my readers to resolve what he would do, had he the power in his own hands to control production and distribution, and was requested to supply sixty or seventy millions of people with the necessities and luxuries of life.

Shut your eyes, and imagine for a moment the whole expanse of these United States swept clean of cities, towns, villages, farm-houses, country roads, fences, and railroads. After you have done this, and have before your mind's eye this virgin field from which to produce the required necessities of this number of people, answer these questions: —

First.—Would you proceed upon present business methods, and scatter your manufacturing plant in thousands of cities and towns, dividing and subdividing each article of manufacture into many different establishments at widely separated points, *or would you bring each separate article of manufacture into single establishments, and all these manufacturing establishments to one centre?*

Second.—Would you, after manufacturing your goods, scatter the population into thousands of cities and towns, and there establish from one to thousands of small distributing stores, *or would you bring the population to one manufacturing centre, and there, in vast emporiums, arrange to distribute the manufactured product?*

Third.—Would you build your homes for each family separate, and compel each family to maintain its own culinary and dining apartments, *or would you bring them together in vast apartment houses, where these departments could be under the control of scientific and intelligent directors, and maintained with the least amount of labor?*

Fourth.—Would you follow the present system of raw production, and scatter twenty millions of our population to live isolated on small farms and in mining sections all over the country, *or would you produce each article from vast tracts that were scientifically known to be best adapted to producing the product desired?*

Fifth.—*Are you not convinced that it is more economical to bring all raw production to one centre of population rather than keep up an exchange system between thousands of cities and towns?*

Sixth.—*Are you not convinced that progress would be more rapid where the people lived in one city, where the educational system would give each an equal opportunity for scientific advancement, and every step of progress, scientific, artistic, and inventive, was before each individual?*

Seventh.—*Would it not be better to make the whole world contribute to the beauty and perfection of one city, there to centre all art and all that contributed to intellectual advancement, rather than spread our wealth and energies over the earth in thousands of cities and towns?*

Eighth.—Would you maintain a system of money, or any representative values, for the purposes of production and distribution, with the enormous expense and labor of maintaining such a system, or would you make all products of the people free, only stipulating that each member of the community should do his portion of labor to maintain such a liberal system?

Leaving my readers to answer these questions to their own satisfaction, and to construct upon the foundation of their own ideas an ideal government, wherein production and distribution would be for-

Google

warded on business principles by the people, on the same economical basis that would be necessary in the individual conduct of any business, I will proceed to give my views, which are based on a firm conviction that rapid progress demands control of production and distribution by the people, centralization of all manufacturing at one central city, and centralization of our population in that city, except those, who, for limited periods, were engaged in the field of raw production or otherwise disposed.

METROPOLIS.

Under a perfect economical system of production and distribution, and a system combining the greatest elements of progress, there can be only one city on a continent, and possibly only one in the world. There would be outlying groups of buildings in different sections of the country for the accommodation of those who were, for limited periods, in the field of labor, and also others that would be occupied as resorts of pleasure in season; but the great and only " Metropolis " would be the home of the people. Having this idea in view, the location of the great city requires thoughtful and careful consideration, it being, in fact, the heart of a vast machine, to which over the thousands of miles of arteries of steel the raw material of production would find its way, there to be transformed in the mammoth mills and workshops into the life-giving elements that would sustain and electrify the mighty brain of the whole, which would be the combined intelligence of the entire population working in unison, but each and every individual working in his own channel of inclination.

For many reasons I have come to the conclusion that there is no spot on the American continent, or possibly in the world, that combines so many natural advantages as that section of our country lying in the vicinity of the Niagara Falls, extending east into New York State and west into Ontario. The possibility of utilizing the enormous natural power resulting from the fall, from the level of Lake Erie to the level of Lake Ontario, some 330 feet, is no longer the dream of enthusiasts, but is a demonstrated fact. Here is a power, which, if brought under control, is capable of keeping in continuous operation every manufacturing industry for centuries to come, and, in addition, supply all the lighting facilities, run all the elevators, and furnish the power necessary for the transportation system of the great central city.

In the utilization of this power, I cannot see that it is necessary to take it from Niagara River. In the first place, the fall between Lake Erie and Ontario is 330 feet; and that section west of Niagara

River lying between the two lakes is a narrow neck of land, which for a distance of forty miles does not average more than thirty miles in width.   It is across this neck that the Welland Canal has been constructed, which, with its twenty-seven locks, allows of the passage of vessels of large tonnage, the entire fall by lockage being 330 feet. Now, it not only seems possible, but a simple engineering feat, to pipe this distance, with intervening falls at turbine stations, for the utilization of the power resulting from the passage of the water through the pipes from the upper to the lower lake.   If the distance were equally divided into ten falls, it would give 30 feet to each fall, and 3 feet fall to the flow between stations.   These pipes could be as large as desired, and only limited in number by the demand of power needed by the various industries of the people; and, eventually, the power now going to waste over the Falls of Niagara would be every pound utilized in its passage through the pipe lines. The Falls of Niagara are only 160 feet high : the fall of water through these pipe lines would be 330 feet.   It is estimated that there is a steady flow of 6,000,000 horse-power over the falls.   The same amount of water passing through these pipe lines would furnish more than twice this amount of power.   One thousand pipe lines, each with a capacity of 10,000 horse-power, would equal 10,000,000 horse-power.   This, reckoned on a basis of cost per horse-power where coal is used, about $15, makes it worth $1,500,-000,000 per year to the people, which would be in largest part a direct saving of labor in mining coal, which it would displace.

The manufacturing industries of "Metropolis" would be located east and west of Niagara River in Ontario and New York.   The residence portion of the city would commence about ten miles east of Niagara River and Buffalo; and from this point to its eastern extremity, which would include the present city of Rochester in its eastern border, the city would be sixty miles long east and west, and thirty miles in width north and south, lying parallel with Lake Ontario, and about five miles from it.

Water for the purposes of the city could be taken from the elevation of Lake Erie, and discharged as waste into Lake Ontario.   As the fall is 330 feet between these two lakes, it is reasonable to suppose that some system might be devised whereby the water required for domestic and city purposes could be made to flow naturally through the city, from one lake to the other, with very little necessity of pumping, and that a large portion of it could be utilized at its outlet to generate power.

Another natural advantage of the section for a great city is the conformation of the land, which is comparatively level through this part of New York State, and well adapted for a city such as described.

For the purpose of more clearly locating "Metropolis" in the minds of my readers, I accompany this description with a map of that portion of New York State and country lying in the vicinity of the falls.   The residence portion of the city is given in dotted out-

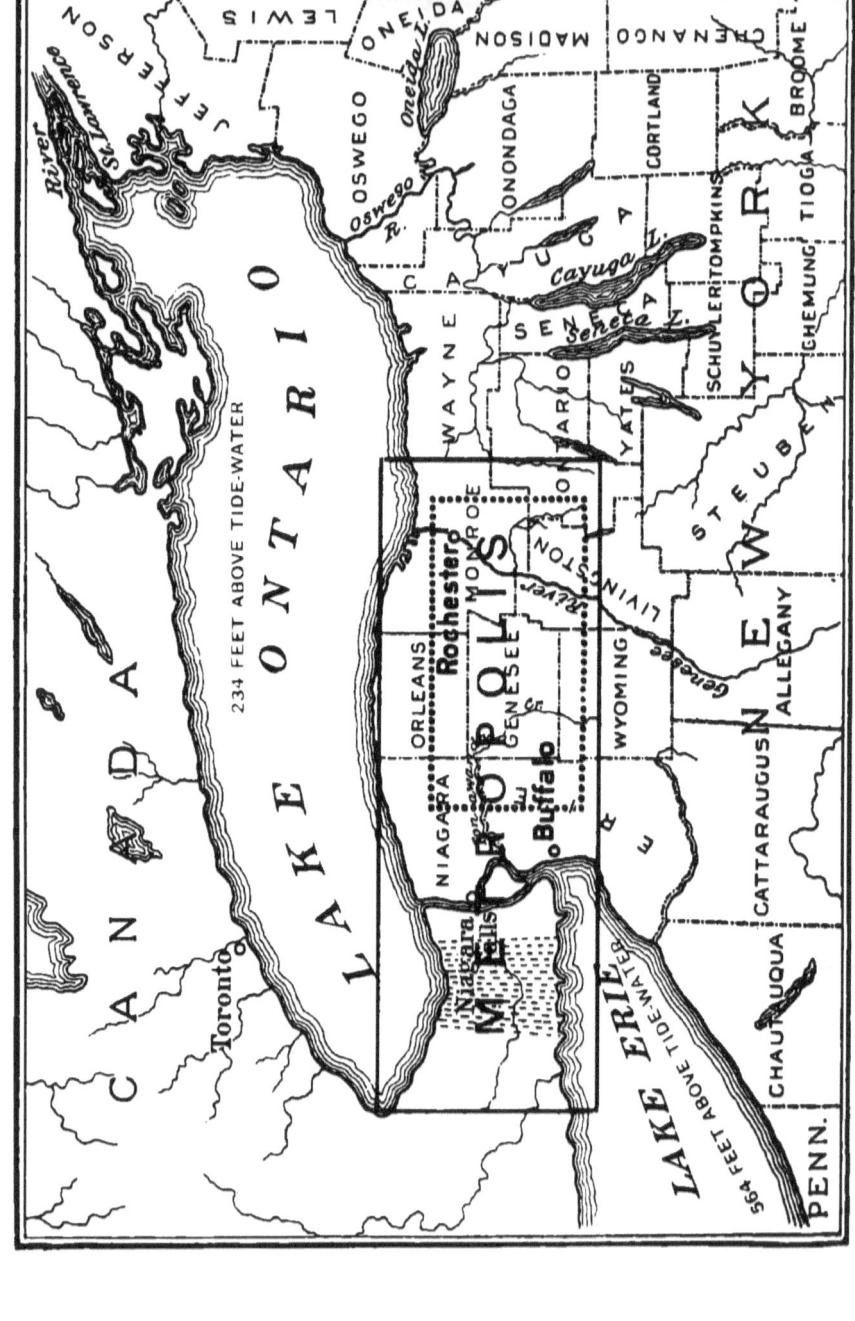

line, and lies south and parallel with Lake Ontario, and takes in, in part, the counties of Niagara, Erie, Orleans, Wyoming, Livingston, Monroe, and Ontario. That section lying between the western boundary of the city and Niagara River and the section immediately west of Niagara River would be utilized for the manufacturing industries of the people. The dotted lines connecting Lakes Erie and Ontario, a distance of from twenty-five to thirty miles, shows the proposed section wherein pipe lines could be laid for the purpose of generating power in the fall of water from Lake Erie to Lake Ontario.

No matter what problems or difficulties confront engineers in thus connecting these two lakes by direct pipe lines, it should be done; for the power thus secured and brought under control for public use would, in the long run, result in an enormous saving of labor over any other possible means of obtaining a like power. Converted into the electric current, it would drive all the machinery of production, and in the form of light convert " Metropolis " into a fairyland.

Here should be located the great central city, which would be the home of all; and to the artistic beauty, grandeur, and magnificence of this wonderful production of the combined intelligence of a united people, the whole world would contribute its wealth and treasures.·

In the building of this great central city, it must be considered in the light of a machine, or rather a part of the machine of production and distribution; and, as such, the objects to be attained must be known and understood. It must have no unnecessary parts to cause friction or demand unnecessary labor, and yet it must combine within itself all the necessary parts which will contribute to the happiness and comfort of all. Under such a system, the people would live in mammoth apartment houses or hotels, and be free from all the annoyances of housekeeping. These apartment buildings would be conducted upon a scale of magnificence such as no civilization has ever known, and would be distributed on a determined plan that would give an average equal population to the square mile throughout the city. The labor incident to the managing and conducting of these apartment buildings on a most liberal basis, as well as labor incident to keeping the city in a condition of cleanliness and beauty, would all be furnished by the Bureau of Labor, the same as other labor would be furnished for the departments of public service. The most magnificent modern hotel in New York could not compare in beauty of its rooms and liberality of its service with any one of these thousands of buildings of "Metropolis." Built in circular form, each would stand a perfect work of art, separate and apart from all surrounding buildings, a distance sufficient to give ample perspective to bring out its beauty as a whole.

In the description here given of " Metropolis," these buildings are separated twelve hundred feet from centre to centre, and the buildings themselves are about six hundred feet in diameter. Thus the nearest point of contact between any two buildings is not less than

·six hundred feet. This arrangement of equal distances from centres, allowing ample space between buildings, which would be laid out in avenues, walks, and gardens, results in a city that is a beautiful park throughout its whole extent. It is calculated that with our present population of seventy million there would be at least sixty million who would occupy this city, while of the balance, ten million, some would be in the field of production, and others travelling for pleasure or occupying apartment houses in the country and along our coast. To accommodate these sixty million people, would require twenty-four thousand apartment buildings, capable of accommodating, on an average, two thousand five hundred persons each, which, distributed on the plan proposed, would result in a city that would cover the distance shown in the dotted outline on the map.

In the building of "Metropolis," the usual plan of construction is departed from. It is laid out, upon a determined plan of equal distribution of population, and the equal distribution of all the requirements of the people; and it would make no difference if the population were one million or one hundred million, the plan of distribution would remain the same, and the city's accommodations would be increased from year to year to meet the requirements of increase of population.

In the construction of this city, durability of structure in every part is of first importance; and to this end steel has been used throughout its entire framework, and brick or terra-cotta is used as the material of greatest safety and durability, in all walls, ceilings, and floors, both the steel framework and the brick being afterward protected and covered from view by a facing of glazed tile or glass in every part of the structure, both inside and outside. *These four great materials, structural steel, fire-brick, glass, and tiling, would constitute the most important industries on which the building of "Metropolis" would depend.*

As, in this description of "Metropolis," I shall advocate the use of porcelain-faced brick or art tile, as the most desirable of all materials as a facing for both interior and exterior finish of all buildings, as well as for pavements, except where glass is used, it may be well to enumerate some of its many advantages.

If properly manufactured and applied (which must be conceded), there can be no question as to the durability of glazed tile; for it is practically indestructible, and there is no material in the world for building purposes that can compare with tiling in its possible range of treatment, both in artistic design and coloring, as well as adaptability to assume any desired form in course of manufacture for panels and mouldings, and for covering pillars, girders, etc.; and for pavements, where traffic vehicles were unknown, it would be clean and durable. Further, it would be one of the cheapest of all known materials from a labor point of view; for, if carried forward on the extensive scale necessary in building such a city, automatic machinery would be quickly adapted to its manufacture, and it would not be long before it would be cheaper than the common plaster on our walls. In "Metropolis" there would be upward of a hundred million rooms; and, of these rooms, hundreds of thousands would be exactly the same in dimensions. Therefore, the same sizes and shapes of tile would be adapted to all these rooms of like dimensions; but in artistic design and coloring there could be an almost endless variety. The possibilities of the development of this art are limitless. The plaster material which is its base can be fashioned into limitless forms, and made to perfectly imitate nature, and combines within its sphere the art of the sculptor, the painter, and the architect. Another and most pertinent reason why glazed tile should excel all other known material, is its absolute cleanliness and non-absorbent qualities, and its power to resist all taint from a diseased and poisoned atmosphere. For these reasons alone, it has already received the indorsement of eminent physicians, and been adopted for the wards in modern hospitals and in some of our public buildings. Only one thing has mitigated against its more general adoption, and this has been its cost; for, as an industry, it is in its infancy, and in each instance of use it has to be adapted to single rooms or single buildings, and made to order. But where it was carried forward on a large scale, and adapted to like conditions in thousands of instances, it would be the cheapest building material in the world, when its beauty and durability were considered.

The architectural plan of "Metropolis" must be carefully considered, and in arriving at the best plan of construction the requirements must be taken in detail.

First.— The city must have a perfect system of sewage of sufficient capacity to carry off all drainage and refuse that must necessarily be a part of such a vast population. This system must be practically indestructible.

Second.— The city must have a perfect system of water distribution. The water must be pure and unlimited in quantity; and the system of pipes must also be indestructible, and be either lined or made of material that will not affect the purity of the water.

Third.— There must be a cold-air distributing system, which is used for cold storage in the food department buildings and for reducing the temperature of dining halls, educational halls, and lecture-rooms wherever aggregations of people make such reduction of temperature desirable during warm weather.

Fourth.— There must be a perfect heat-distributing system, by which every apartment and every public building can be maintained at an equable temperature. This might possibly be electrical, if the progress of this science should demonstrate its economy.

Fifth.— There must be a perfect system of transportation, by which each building where food is prepared is supplied with its proportion of all food products.

Sixth.— There must be a perfect system of electric telephonic communication between every apartment in this vast city, so that it will be possible for any two apartments to instantly come into communication with each other, or with any of the public buildings of the city, or with any of its manufacturing establishments, or with any place or individual within the environment of North America.

In the building of "Metropolis" there would be no excavating for sewage, heating, cold air, and electric systems. Each would be above ground and in plain sight, where every defect could be noted and repairs made without unnecessary labor. To accomplish this, a chamber is formed above ground by the erection of steel pillars and the building of a platform throughout the length and breadth of the city. The pillars used are of such different height as to overcome the inequalities of land surface, and make it possible to lay a perfectly level platform at the top of the pillars, it being calculated to be elevated at least twenty-five feet from the ground. This platform is composed of frameworks of steel inlaid with glass, similar to the numerous vault lights of our cities, which admit light to cellars and basements. We now have a perfectly level floor of glass and steel throughout the city, and the chamber beneath that platform is as light as day.

After further consideration it was thought that a similar chamber constructed in same manner above this first chamber would be the easiest and most effective manner of providing for the transportation system. So, again, the steel pillars come into play, and a second platform is constructed twenty-five feet above the first platform. It was now determined that the easiest way to provide the people with shelter in passing from one building to another or about the city in inclement weather, could be secured by the formation of a third chamber. This was determined on, and again the steel pillars rise, this time to a height of fifty feet above the second platform, and at the top of these pillars the third and last platform is built. All of these three platforms extend throughout the length and breadth of the city like level floors, a large portion of each surface being of glass.

The buildings of the city have their foundation in the ground, but the buildings proper rise above the upper platform. The people do not feel conscious of the elevation above the surrounding country; for the platforms, in anticipation of the city's growth, extend out beyond the city proper beyond the range of vision. There is absolutely no way by which dirt or dust can find its way into the city in any appreciable amount. There are no traffic vehicles of any kind in the city except the electric transportation system of the middle chamber and rubber-tired electrical carriages and bicycles.

In the construction of "Metropolis," the walls of all buildings could be of one thickness, from the bottom to the top. This would be made possible by supporting the weight of each story on independent girders, that would be securely fastened to the upright pillars which would have their foundation in the ground.

The design and specifications of every building would be made the subject of competition between the architects of the country, the same being submitted to the Bureau of Architecture, who would pass upon their labor, and award the credit. The incentive given to this branch of public welfare would make architecture, in all its details, one of the most fascinating scientific studies, and would result in an endless variety of beautiful designs, both in exterior and interior finish of buildings. This would give perpetual beauty and variety to the city as a whole.

Each apartment of all buildings would be supplied with every convenience of modern science, art, and invention,— heated and cooled by automatic mechanism, lighted by electricity, and electrically connected with the whole outside world ; and supplied with an unfailing supply of pure water.

The ground, or lower, chamber of the city, which contained the various pipe and wire systems, would be treated in white only, the ground being first covered with a cement or asphalt composition, and then a layer of white glazed tiling. The girders and pillars of this chamber would also be covered with white tile designed expressly for this purpose.

The second, or middle, chamber would contain the transportation facilities of the city, which would connect with every building, both for the convenience of the people and for the purpose of delivering food products to the culinary departments. This chamber would also be treated in white tiling, relieved by colored borders.

The upper chamber, fifty feet in height, would be a bewildering scene of beauty in its artistic treatment. The floors, ceiling, and pillars of porcelain tile, with their ever-changing variety in colors and designs, the artificial parks topped above the upper platform with domes of colored glass in beautiful designs, its urns of flowers, and beautiful works of art and statuary, would make it an endless gallery of loveliness. Here would be found a panorama of beauty that would throw into shadow the fables of wonderful palaces and cities told of in the "Arabian Nights"; yet the genii of all this would be naught but the intelligence of man working in unison. What would be seen here is within our knowledge to do, and with less expenditure of labor than is now required to maintain our present cities.

The upper, or outdoor, pavement would be tile and glass throughout its length and breadth. Here the pavement would be subdued in coloring and in dead finish, but would be practically without limit in its variety of color and designs. This upper pavement and the upper chamber would both offer an endless vista of beauty for the pedestrian, the bicyclist, and those who use electric carriages. At night the upper chamber, the upper pavement, and the interior courts and domes would be brilliant with a flood of electric light which would throw into soft relief the beauties of environment, and make of the whole, a fairyland.

That my readers may better understand the general plan of "Metropolis," I have prepared a series of plates and appended descriptions, which will enable them to form a mental picture of the city as a whole.

The map, showing location of city, has already been referred to, and a general idea of location is understood.

FLATE I.

PLAN OF DISTRIBUTION OF BUILDINGS IN THE PROPOSED CENTRAL CITY.

PLATE I.

Plate I. is a small section of the plan of the great central city "Metropolis," and shows the means whereby the population and the necessary adjuncts of civilization would be equally distributed.

This small section shown in the plate contains thirty-three apartment buildings, five educational buildings, marked A, five amusement buildings, marked B, and five buildings where food is stored and prepared, marked C.

It will be noticed by reference to plan of distribution of buildings, that each A, B, and C building is the centre of six surrounding apartment buildings, and therefore contributes to the requirements of the population of these six buildings.

It will be further noticed that each apartment building is central in its relation to each necessary building A, B, and C.

The section shown is a little more than two square miles in area, and shows the arrangement of buildings, their relation to each other, and the plan of division of the outdoor space into lawns, avenues, walks, etc. Each building is six hundred feet distant at nearest point of contact with those surrounding it. This allows for an artificial lawn of one hundred and fifty feet in width around each building, with a glass and porcelain walk of one hundred and fifty feet between. These walks, being straight, would leave a triangular space between the junctions of any three roads. This triangle of about three hundred feet would be covered, in part, with glass, in dome shape, to give light to the walks and chamber below the upper pavement. These walks below would correspond with the walks above, while the triangular space below the glass dome in the upper chamber would be a park or conservatory of flowers.

Of these conservatories there would be thirty-six thousand in a city of sixty million population. Here flowers would bloom at every season of the year. There would also be trees and urns of flowers distributed at regular intervals along both sides and through the centre of every walk of the city, both on the upper platform and in the chamber below.

As the population increased, there would be a proportionate increase and extension of the city's accommodations; and these accommodations would always keep a little in advance of actual requirements. Thus, if they kept five or ten per cent. in advance of population in buildings, there would always be a large surplus of unoccupied apartments distributed throughout the city in the different buildings. This would always give the individual a wide range of choice of location of apartments and opportunities to change, if desired.

PLATE II.

SHOWING PLAN OF A SINGLE APARTMENT BUILDING AND ITS SURROUNDINGS.

a Tiers of apartments.
b Inner court formed by the connecting of tiers of apartments, in form of a circle.
c Dining-room in center of court.
d Lawns surrounding buildings.
e Walks 50 ft. wide leading from buildings to avenues.
f Avenues 150 ft. wide.
g Glass domes, 200 ft. on each side, rising to a height of 100 ft. These domes give light to chamber below, and are directly over park in triangle form, that is 350 ft. on each side.
h Is lawn surrounding dome of glass, thereby giving a continuous border of green to every avenue in the city.

PLATE II.

The apartment building shown in Plate II. is designed to be six hundred feet in diameter, twenty-five stories in height, and consists of eighteen tiers of apartments, so arranged and connected at the back that it makes a single building in circular form, with an interior court four hundred and fifty feet in diameter, the central portion of which is occupied by a dining-room that is two hundred and fifty feet in diameter.

The triangular spaces shown at the intersection of avenues, six of which surround each building, are domes of glass surrounded by a lawn.

The lawns surrounding each building are in hexagonal shape on their outer circumference, average about one hundred and fifty feet in width, and, following line of avenues, are about one-half mile in circumference.

These lawns would be laid out in shrubbery, beds of flowers interspersed with statues, fountains, and beautiful works of art. Can you imagine the endless beauty of a conception like this,— a city with its thirty-six thousand buildings each a perfectly distinct and complete design, with a continuous and perfectly finished façade from every point of view, each building and avenue surrounded and bordered by an ever-changing beauty in flowers and foliage? There would be in this city of sixty million souls fifteen thousand miles of main avenues, every foot of which would be a continuous change of beauty.

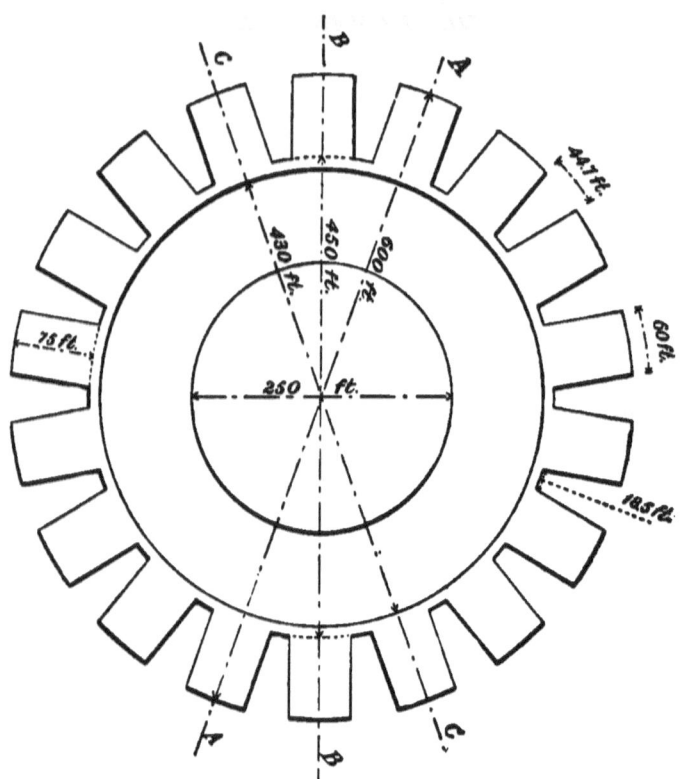

PLATE III.

PLAN OF APARTMENT BUILDING.

A Diameter of building over all, 600 ft.
B Diameter of court from apartment to apartment, 450 ft.
C Diameter of court from inner point of landing at each story, 430 ft.
Dining-room occupying central part of court, 250 ft.
Apartments, 60 x 75 ft.
Space between apartments on outer face, 44.7 ft.
Space between apartments where they join, 18.5 ft.

(98)

PLATE III.

Plate III. gives a general idea of the floor plan of an apartment building. Being circular in outline and distant from other buildings, it has every facility for light and ventilation, and every apartment is made equally desirable.

In effect, apartment buildings built on this plan consist of a series of tall buildings joined together at the back, and forming, as a whole, a mammoth circular building, with an interior court several hundred feet in diameter, surmounted by a dome.

In my plate and description I have adhered to a single plan; but the reader will readily understand, that, while retaining outline, size, and contour of building in general, there will be limitless possibilities in designs of buildings and arrangement of interiors.

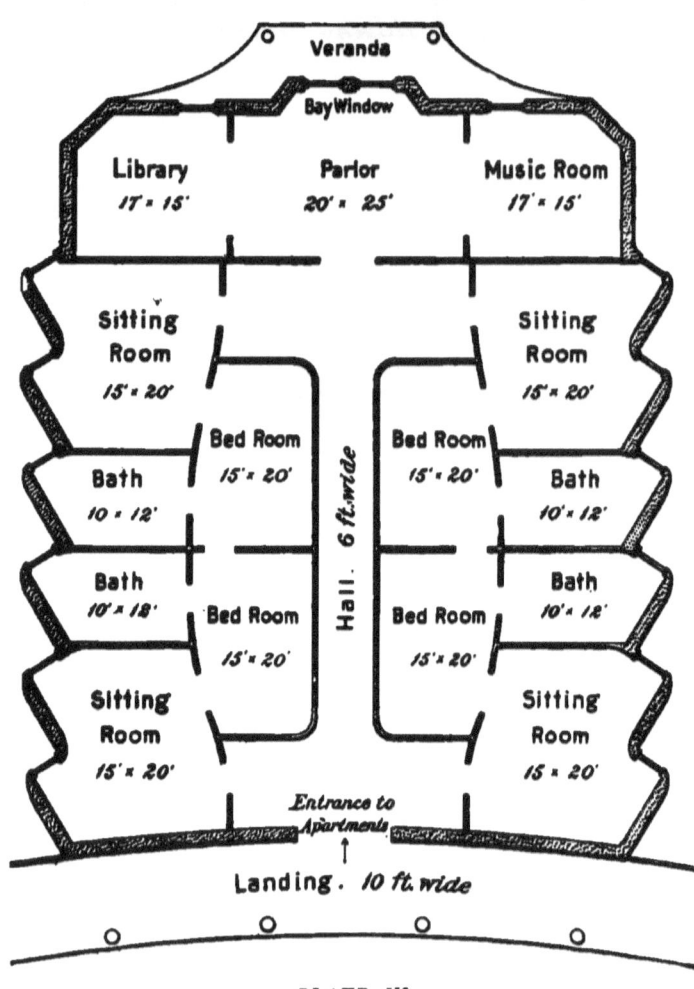

PLATE IV.

FLOOR PLAN OF A SINGLE APARTMENT.

(100)

PLATE IV.

Plate IV. represents the floor plan of a family apartment designed to accommodate from four to eight persons.

Across the front the apartment is taken up with parlor, library, and music-room. Back of this are four complete suites of rooms, consisting of sitting-room, bedroom, and bath, all on a liberal scale as to size.

The windows of these rooms are so arranged that they look out and away from the building, which makes it impossible to look from one apartment into an opposite one.

The space between apartments has been calculated on such a liberal scale that each apartment is practically the same as a detached dwelling.

It is of course understood that there would be a large variety in size and variation of these floor plans, to accommodate any number of persons, from a single individual up to the largest family, each flat or apartment being complete in number of suites of rooms to meet requirements.

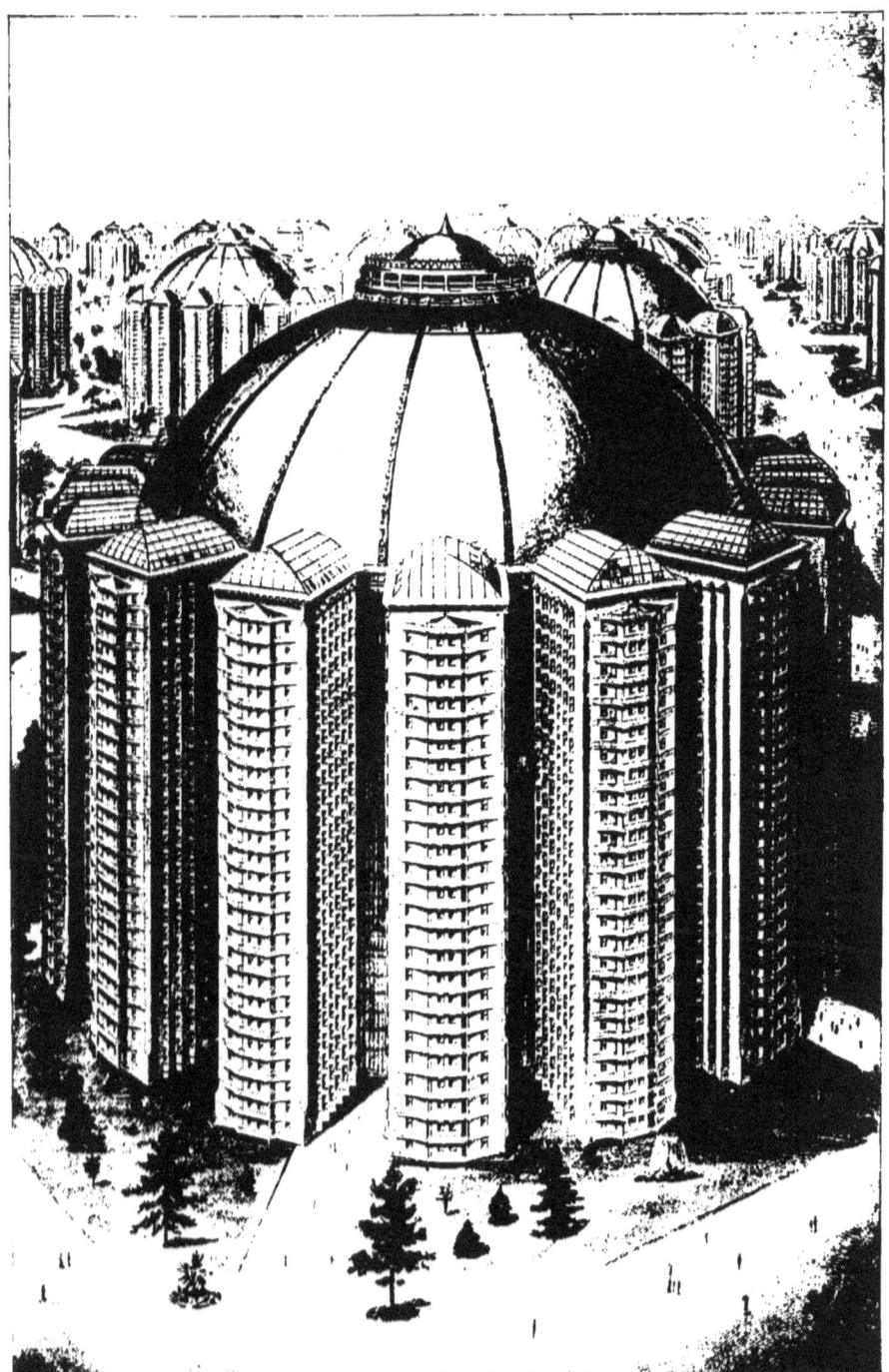

PLATE V

PLATE V.

Plate V. gives a perspective view of a complete building and its imaginary surroundings.   Here we see the tiers of apartments arranged in a circle and joined at the back, and the interior court thus formed is surmounted by a dome of metal and glass.

The windows on the sides of apartments are so constructed that they will look out and away from the building.

The space between tiers of apartments on outer face is about forty-five feet.   At the back the space is about eighteen feet.   The connecting walls at back of tiers of apartments are of metal and ground or colored glass, which will admit sufficient light to the interior court without admitting the glare and heat of the sun.   In this space in the back the elevators of the building are seen.

If you can take a building such as described, twenty-five stories in height, and spread it in imagination over a ground space twenty-five times as great, you can get some idea of the ground space saved in building up instead of spreading out.

With the modern convenience of express elevators that are absolutely safe, and rise almost as swift as an arrow, there would be little choice between the lower and upper apartments of a twenty-five story building.

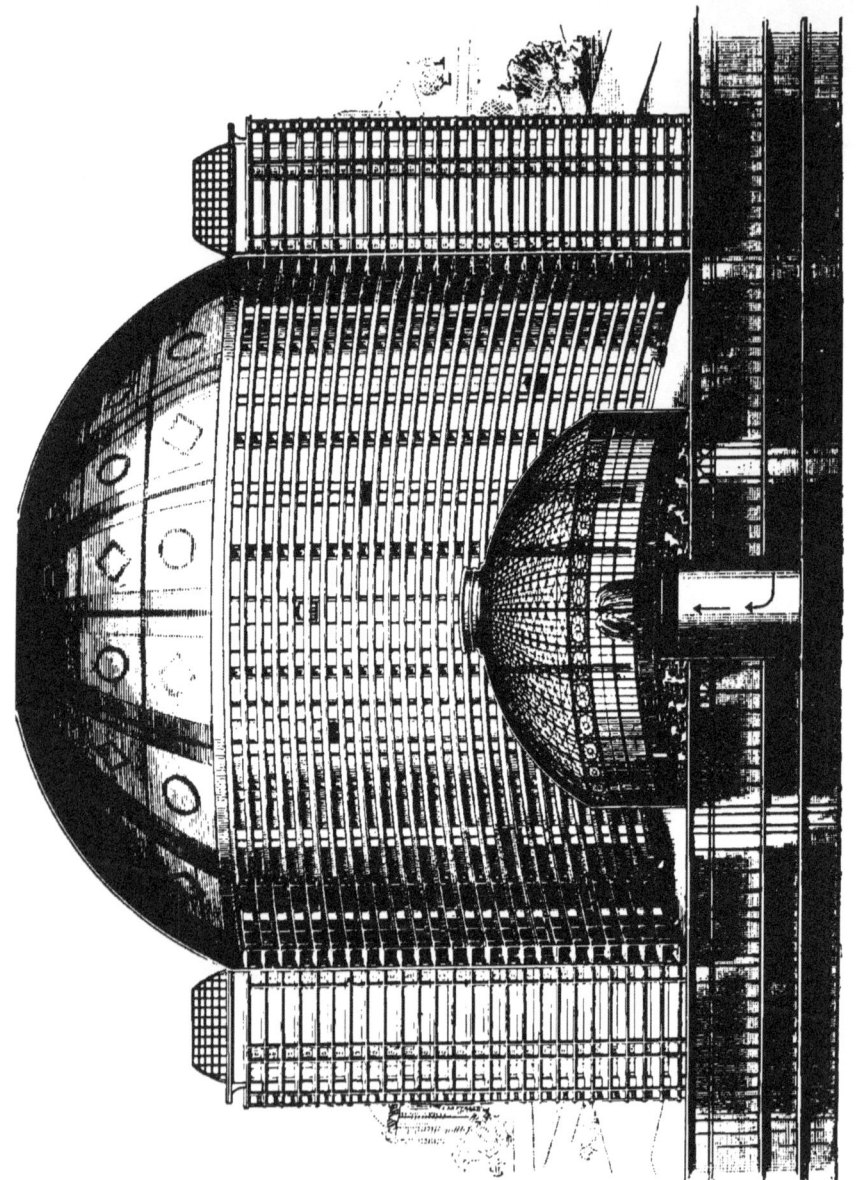

PLATE VI.

PLATE VI.

Plate VI. gives a sectional interior view of this same building. This view is not intended to convey any idea of artistic finish, but merely to give a general idea of construction. In this view, also, the three underlying chambers of the city are shown. A, being the lower or ground chamber, is utilized for sewage, water, hot and cold air, and electric systems ; B, the middle chamber, is utilized for the transportation system ; and C, the upper chamber, fifty feet in height, is for the purpose of giving additional room and facilities for the people in moving about, and would be especially desirable in inclement weather.

In the plate the location of dining-room in central part of court is shown. Food would find its way to these dining-rooms from the building where it was prepared, by an electric transfer system, something on the same principle as now employed in the transfer of money in our large emporiums. This system need take up but little room, and could be laid close to the ceiling of middle chamber. The time of transit of food-carrier from the building where food would be prepared to the dining-rooms, a distance of about one thousand feet, would probably be less than ten seconds.

Galleries ten feet wide surround the court at each story, from which access is had to the different apartments.

Imagine for a moment the possibilities in light and color when these immense courts were brilliant with thousands of electric lights, and the interior of the large domes decorated with exquisite paintings that would be the result of inspiration.

Of all the thirty to forty thousand buildings in the city, no two need be alike in artistic treatment.

PLATE VII.

Plate VII. shows a single tier of apartments in process of construction, with the different platforms that extend throughout the length and breadth of the city, broken away in part, so as to show the extension and construction of the supporting columns of the building.

These buildings are constructed upon the general plan of modern office buildings, such as are seen in cities like Chicago, New York, etc. It consists of a steel framework that is filled in between its network of beams and girders with fire brick, which constitutes floors and walls. These floors and walls are then covered by a facing of porcelain tile in every part of the building, both inside and out.

The weight of successive stories does not come upon the stories below, but are each separately supported upon independent steel beams or girders, that are fastened to the uprights of the building; and there each independently contributes its weight, these uprights being calculated in strength to support the weight of the building. By this plan the thickness of the walls of the lower story are exactly the thickness of the walls of the upper story, and this thickness is only sufficient to meet the requirements of insulation under varying degrees of temperature.

The building, though apparently rising from the upper platform, in reality rises from the ground one hundred feet below, where it gets its foundation and support.

A building built as described would be practically indestructible, and I doubt if one thousand years would impair its usefulness or beauty. If this be true, and the cost were divided among the successive generations who would live in a single apartment, how little would be the proportionate labor of each in contributing to the construction of such a home !

A city on this plan could be forwarded very rapidly, for the duplication of framework would make it possible to utilize special machinery in the steel mills for turning out special parts. It is only necessary to calculate the amount of labor required to erect a single tier of apartments, to soon know the labor and time required to erect thousands of buildings of like or nearly like construction.

The same sewage system which would apply to one group of buildings would only need to be multiplied to apply it to all similar groups. This applies also to the water, telegraph, telephone, general electric, cold air, heat-distributing and transportation systems.

Here we have a city every building of which is a perfect work of art, and whose setting is nature's loveliest handiwork, made perfect by the intelligence of man.

How can we believe for a moment that we are now securing the best results of our highest intelligence, when we have it in our power to live in places such as described, and are yet content to crowd ourselves in cities where the streets are narrow, filthy, and ill-paved, where not a blade of grass or a single flower is seen except in isolated parks and a few florists' windows, and where millions live who never inhale the fragrance of nature's purest loveliness?

It does not follow that if a city were laid out regularly, it would necessarily become monotonous from sameness. Although the buildings and population would be equally distributed, and each building designed to accommodate about the same number, here all similarity would end; for the beauty of environment would change with almost every move of the beholder. The eye could not rest on any two buildings that were alike in architecture, in design, or in coloring. Each and every building of "Metropolis" would be a complete and distinct work of art in itself. Every color and every shade of color would be found in their ceramic treatment. In some instances, there would be a gradual dissolving from a dark shade of color at the base to an almost white at the top of the buildings. In others, the general dissolving of one tint into another would give an effect that would combine all the prismatic tints of the rainbow. In others, a single delicate tint would be the predominating feature. Here, one would look as though chiselled from a block of emerald, another from jet, another from turquoise, and another from amethyst. One would have metallic lustre tints, while others would combine kaleidoscopic effects in colors and designs. Some would vie with nature in their beautiful designs in flowers; and, again, the most beautiful results could be produced in the opalescent effects that would result from the application of combinations of colors in fine grooves, which could only be seen at the proper angle of observation. With every move of the individual, a transformation would take place. One tint would gradually dissolve through many shades into a different color. Pink would fade into green, green into gold; red, through every shade of purple, to blue, and so on through endless combinations; and with every change of reflected light, there would be a dissolving and gradual change in the beauties around us. *We can never obtain grand effects in architecture except by ample space and complete conceptions in buildings.*

Perspective is as necessary to artistic expression of architecture as proportion and design. A building that is high and broad should have an open space around it, sufficient to allow of its beauty being grasped as a whole; and a building should be built in such outline, and so removed from other buildings, that it has a continuous and harmonious façade from every point of view. This is not possible in the construction of buildings in our present cities. Our modern office buildings are the result of necessity; and the architect, instead of being allowed the free play of his imagination in the development of an artistic conception, is obliged to make his ideas conform to a contracted and narrow strip of land on which to build, not a building, but a tower.

Imagine for a moment these thirty odd thousand buildings of "Metropolis," each standing alone, a majestic work of art,—a city which, with our present population, would be from sixty to seventy-five miles in length, and twenty to thirty in width,— a never-ending city of beauty and cleanliness, and then compare it with our cities of filth, crime, and misery, with their ill-paved and dirty thoroughfares, crowded with the struggling masses of humanity and the system of necessary traffic. And then compare the machinery of both systems, and take your choice; for I believe the only obstacle that lies in the way of the building of this great city is man. For, if he chooses to build it, he has the necessary intelligence, and can complete it within twenty-five years. The same endless variety in colors and designs would be found in the treatment of interiors; but in the ceramic decoration of upward of one hundred million rooms, it would be possible to use the same designs in different colors and combinations of borders and panels in hundreds of thousands of rooms, and yet no two rooms would be treated exactly alike. It would be only natural that there would be hundreds of thousands, possibly millions, of rooms of exactly the same dimensions; and thus machinery would economically come into play where such a wide field of duplication was possible. This is why I assert that tiling, though expensive now as a decorative feature of buildings, would, under these conditions of production, be actually cheaper than the common plaster on our walls. My idea is that the city should be actually a city of porcelain, as far as outside appearance was concerned, except where glass was used, and where wood or metal was used for window frames and doors.

I wish to speak here of another advantage which would result from there being millions of rooms of the same dimensions. In the manufacturing department of "Metropolis" rugs and carpets would be one of the large industries; and, where there were millions of rooms of like dimensions, it would be possible to make special machinery to weave carpets or rugs to the exact dimensions of rooms. In cases where millions were to be made to the same dimensions there could be thousands of different designs and combinations and shades of coloring.

THE MANUFACTURING CENTRE.

It is now my purpose to describe in outline that portion of " Metropolis " where the manufacturing industries of the people would be carried forward. This portion of the city would lie east of the Niagara River, but might be extended west of the river, should Canada and the United States join hands in the common purpose. The manufacturing and residence portion of the city would be connected by a continuation of the three platforms, which would be the same in all sections of the city, and which would also be continued in the form of bridges over the river.

The same idea of durability in all structural work would be maintained in the manufacturing portion of the city, the only difference being in general design of buildings, which would be adapted in each instance, in size and convenience to the industrial purpose carried forward within its walls, and would, in each separate case, form a geometrical part of the machine of production. Each building would stand separate and apart from all others, and liberal space would be allowed for their necessary future extension.

The same artistic beauty would be maintained in the exterior architectural design of the buildings and in the upper chamber and outdoor platform of this portion of the city.

In interior arrangement, ample room would be allowed, so there would be no crowding of machinery or lack of room for handling material, and every facility for light and ventilation would be provided for. In general, white porcelain would be used for floors, ceilings, and walls, relieved to a limited extent by colored borders and panels of beautiful design.

The machinery in every establishment would be made as nearly automatic in the handling of material as possible, as well as handling material to and from machines and from one machine to another, and to and from the transportation system, which would find entrance beneath each building. This automatic system would be made a distinctive feature, which would prove practical where material was handled in large quantity ; and constant and rapid progress would be made in this direction.

All machines would be run by the direct application of electric power, all shafting and belting being dispensed with wherever it was practicable.

The general working of this industrial system, by which the vast population would be supplied with every material want, would be simplicity itself, and would combine order and economy in every part. The raw material, brought from every section of America or foreign lands, would be delivered in cars direct to that establishment where it was to be utilized in the process of manufacture. Here the wheat would be delivered to the mill direct from the field where it was produced ; and it would be the same with wool, cotton, hides, and spices from foreign lands, and the hundreds of items that go to swell the demand of a large population. Articles of food consumption would be produced with the greatest care, and the highest standard of quality and purity would always be maintained; and there would be a constant gain in this direction.

The manufactured product, in its finished state, would be delivered from the machines into packages containing from five hundred pounds to a carload; and for special articles used in large quantities, porcelain-lined cars would be provided. In this shape, flour, and many other articles, would be delivered to the storerooms of those buildings of "Metropolis" where food would be prepared, and there remain until contents were used. The whole process of handling food products finds its greatest economy by being thus handled direct from factory to place of consumption in bulk, dispensing entirely with our present system of small packages, which entails an enormous amount of labor. The same principle of handling in bulk would be adhered to in the handling of preserved fruits and vegetables, which would be put up in porcelain-lined packages holding from one hundred to five hundred pounds, such packages being returned to the manufacturing department over and over again.

All manufactured food and products would find their way direct from their place of manufacture to a common centre of distribution, and from this centre they would be distributed to those buildings of "Metropolis" where food was prepared for the table. As I have before described, there are four thousand of these buildings in "Metropolis"; and, at first sight, it might seem like an enormous task to keep them supplied with food from day to day. But, when it is considered that almost all manufactured products could be delivered in quantity sufficient to last a year, it only means the supply of twelve or fourteen of these buildings on an average each day. All such materials as flour, sugar, salt, spices, baking-powder, extracts, soaps, vinegar, syrups, etc., could be delivered in bulk, and in special cars which would be retained in the storerooms of the buildings where the food was prepared until emptied, when they would be returned to the proper manufacturing establishment, and refilled.

The departments devoted to the manufacture of wearing apparel and household necessities would be carried forward on the same general plan, except that the finished product goes direct from the manufacturing establishments to mammoth emporiums. Thus we would have a furniture emporium, rug emporium, curtains and hangings, gentlemen's clothing, underwear, etc., women's dress goods, etc. In these mammoth establishments, would be arranged, in attractive display, the products of the highest developed intelligence in art and science,— goods in greatest variety of texture, design, and beauty, all of highest grade and quality. Here the people would select what they desired *without money and without price.*

Many will maintain that the people would abuse this privilege, but such would not be the case; for under a state of material equality there is no incentive to hoard up, and no one would load themselves down with the care of clothes which they did not need and could not wear. And no one would fill their apartments with a lot of useless trash and furniture which is neither useful nor ornamental, and would be in the way.

I here reiterate what I have said before, that *no system can ever be a perfect system, and free from incentive for crime, until money and all representative value of material is swept from the face of the earth.*

In addition to those manufacturing industries which would contribute directly to the supply of material necessities, would be the mechanical industries,— mammoth machine-shops where machinery would be produced, founderies and rolling mills, and those establishments which contributed to the arts and sciences, to the extension and furtherance of public improvements, and to agricultural implements and machines.

In the generation of the power to meet all the requirements of the people, that which demanded the least manual labor for a given output of energy would be the system adopted. This, without question, would be that which would result from the fall of water from Lake Erie to Lake Ontario. From thousands of turbines this power would be immediately transformed into electrical energy ; and, thus handled, the power would be transmitted direct to the various places where it was to be utilized. Thus from the mammoth electric plant would radiate the energy that was to run the five hundred thousand passenger elevators of " Metropolis," the transportation system, the heat and lighting system, and the mammoth mills, machine-shops, and manufacturing establishments. Like the heart of a sentient being the city would pulsate with life through its millions of arteries of copper and steel, and stand a living, breathing monument of man's combined and highest intelligence.

I believe, as much as I believe that I live, that, if the plan outlined could be understood by the masses, enthusiasm would amount to such a pitch in the excitement and desire to see " Metropolis" completed that millions would enlist their services for an indefinite time to forward its building, and all they would ask would be soldier's fare and clothing. What would money be to them, when the near future would see it pass into the oblivion of an ignorant age ?

AGRICULTURE.

In the field of agriculture, a united people would create a revolution as sweeping in its change from present methods as has been seen in the manufacturing industries, and the saving in labor and material would be fully as great.

Under our present system, our country is divided into innumerable small farms and gardens ; and these, again, are divided into small sections for the production of different articles of consumption. There is no intelligent direction as to how much of any given article is produced ; and, as a result, supply and demand are at continual war with each other, which causes fluctuations in prices and gives rise to speculation.

It would take a volume in itself to enumerate one-half the disadvantages which the public labor under from this system of small farms. In the first place, a more extravagant system could not be devised for supplying a large population with food products. The amount of labor expended in the erection of millions of houses, barns, and necessary buildings, the erection and maintenance of millions of miles of fencing, and the maintenance of upward of a million of miles of country roads, is enough to appall an economist or thinking man, when he sifts the matter down. When he thinks of all these buildings and fences going to decay, these roads needing constant repair, and the superabundance of machinery, tools, and wagons that go to rot, rust, and ruin from disuse; when he thinks of the maintenance of millions of horses that are more than two-thirds of the time idle, and the enormous loss of time and labor of hauling goods to market towns,—when he thinks of all this, it begins to dawn on the mind that there is something radically wrong in our method of raw production.

But these are not the worst features of this divided system of raising food products. We have millions of families and farm hands who are practically isolated from the world and from each other. This system of isolation has a tendency to keep men ignorant, for it will be generally conceded that the broader the field of association between minds, the brighter they become, and isolation, such as is the case with the farmers, goes to the other extreme, and has a tendency to retard the development of the mind.

A united people would place the necessary labor in the field of raw production; but it would not be a permanent, isolated class, for they would only remain in the field as long as their labor was actually required. It would not be necessary to remain to watch the wheat grow, nor after it was harvested. Every branch of agriculture would have its times of labor; but these times of actual labor necessary to any product are, at most, only a small portion of a year, and it would be no part of the work of a united people to sit down beside the tree, and wait for the fruit to ripen.

All products would be produced from vast tracts, such tracts being selected in each instance for their particular fitness to give best results, soil, climate, and conformation of land being considered. The seed would be supplied by the Bureau of Agriculture, and would be the result of careful selection from the crop of the previous year or from the experimental farms of the people, which would be under the supervision of this bureau. The result of this would be a continual development along the whole line of agricultural products both in quality and quantity produced per acre. The possibilities of improvement in agricultural products is without limit; but rapid progress in this field requires scientific and intelligent direction. This great industry should be under the control of the most intelligent, most scientific, and most progressive bureau of men and women that the country could produce.

The good or bad condition of a crop would not depend on the field laborers. Their work would be mechanical: the Bureau of Agriculture would furnish the brains. As a sample of how this would work, let us take a single product, wheat. In considering the production of this necessary product, soil and climate would be the first consideration, next conformation of land ; for, if we want to take advantage of labor-saving machinery in the production of grains, we must have land practically level for long distances. Having decided the amount of product desired for consumption, the land necessary to produce same is selected. At the present time the actual consumption is less than three hundred million bushels. If we place it at three hundred million bushels, and put the average yield, under favorable conditions, at twenty bushels per acre, it would require fifteen million acres to produce the required amount. This would be fifteen tracts, each forty miles square. On these fifteen tracts would thus be produced an equivalent of what is now produced in not less than three hundred thousand separate fields. Under the plan proposed, that of producing the different products of agriculture in vast tracts, I believe there are possibilities of invention in labor-saving machinery to do the different stages of labor that are beyond our present comprehension, and which, under the present system of small farms, would be wholly impracticable. But, even with our present progressive position as regards labor-saving machinery, there would be a vast saving in utilizing same in vast tracts over the present system.

Having selected the necessary tracts, either a temporary building or a permanent one would be erected for the accommodation of those who are supposed to do the necessary labor of agriculture. Or it might be found possible to supply all the needs of an army of laborers by making the transportation system combine hotel accommodations, and thus support the moving army at all times. To the field of labor the army of workers go, accompanied by a necessary complement of those who prepare their food. These laborers would be in sufficient number to do the necessary work in a few days. After the operation of putting wheat in ground had been accomplished, this army would move at once to other fields of agriculture; and, when the wheat was ready to harvest, this or another army of laborers would again occupy the field and do the necessary work. All the operations of the field laborers would be directed by the Bureau of Agriculture, through competent superintendents and foremen. This bureau would have at all times a complete knowledge and control of the whole agricultural field. It would have its special agents in the different sections, who would report at regular intervals the condition of crops, and give notice when additional labor was required. This system would apply to every agricultural product,—grains, vegetables, fruits, cotton, etc. The principle of selecting soil and climate best adapted to each product, and the careful selection of seed, must necessarily result in a higher standard of excellence from year to year, and a more uniform quality. The

Bureau of Agriculture would combine the matured minds of those who had made agriculture a life study. Can any one say, with such a prospect in view, which is perfectly feasible, that it is desirable to continue our present agricultural method, which has little system or order?

A united people, in entering the field of agriculture, would do so by a gradual process of absorption on the same principle as would be adopted in the invasion of the field of manufacture and distribution. First, it would acquire the necessary land to produce the wheat. From this, it would gradually branch out into other fields. By this means, it would grow up to a final control without causing unnecessary confusion; and, when it did finally gain control, it would have every part a perfect working mechanism the same as an individual who starts with a small capital, and finally grows up to a business where he has millions at his command and thousands in his employ. It is just as easy for him to run the large business as it was the small one.

This system of agriculture, in combination with the system of manufacture and distribution and a great central city, is, I believe, the future destiny of this country; for it is the final logical conclusion of economy in production and distribution. *It is the final application of the stock company system to production and distribution as a whole*, which will result in a perfect control of supply and demand.

For the purpose of making the subject more clearly understood, I will say that " Metropolis " would be our home, and North America our farm. From this home, which would combine our highest intelligence in architecture and construction, as well as the accumulated wealth of art and refinement, we would direct and control the whole field of production. From this centre, would radiate the numerous arteries of commerce, which would penetrate every desirable field of production, from which every wagon road would be obliterated, and the railroad made the only avenue of transportation and commerce. We would thus penetrate the wheat-fields of Manitoba, Dakota, Minnesota, and Nebraska; the corn-fields of Kansas and Indian Territory; the cotton-fields of Texas and Louisiana; the orange groves of Florida; the vineyards and fruit-laden districts of California, Ohio, Michigan, New York, New Jersey, and Delaware; the early fruit and vegetable districts of the South, and the later ones of the North; and the tropical districts of Mexico and Central America. But we would not be limited to the products of our own country, for from our ports of entry at New York, San Francisco, and New Orleans we would send our ships laden with products for exchange to foreign lands, and thus secure such as were not indigenous to our soil and climate. *Thus we would have a daily menu that would only be limited in variety and quality by the world's product.*

Under the directing power of the Bureau of Agriculture, this whole field would be under perfect systematic control, as much so as any stock company or corporate interests. They would have a recorded knowledge of every square mile in North America,— its conformation, its climate, and its soil. They would know exactly for what products it was best adapted, and they would know the exact condition and progress of every product at every stage of its growth.

It may be argued by some, that while wheat might be readily produced in this manner, it would not be practical to so produce fruits and vegetables. I will venture to say that it is just as practicable to produce potatoes, onions, and cabbages, as well as currants, strawberries, peaches, and grapes, in extensive tracts, as it is to produce wheat, corn, or cotton; and the saving in the one instance would be fully as great as in the other.

The drawback against producing strawberries on a tract of land of thousands of acres, under our present system, is the impossibility in country districts of obtaining sufficient help at necessary times to do required labor. As a result, before a part of the crop was harvested, the rest would be over-ripe and spoiled. This difficulty would not be present under a united system; for, on one day's notice from the field inspectors, a sufficient force could be placed in a ten-thousand-acre tract of strawberries to harvest it within a week, or within a day, if necessary. This would be true of all small fruits and vegetables; and our army of field laborers would be continually on the move, under the direction of the Bureau of Agriculture.

In addition to the production of products in their regular seasons, there would be thousands of acres under glass in different sections of North America, and it would not be long before the table would be supplied with fresh vegetables and fruit of every variety at all seasons.

On both sides of our trunk line of transportation, for a distance of a mile in width, and along their whole length, could be planted continuous belts of fruit-trees. Thus we would find the ripening of the fruits from the South to the North a continual process throughout long seasons. This same process would be largely adhered to in the production of vegetables and small fruits, especially of those of a perishable nature.

Can any one say that such a system would be impracticable? If there be such an individual, let me ask him what plan he would adopt if he were requested to supply sixty million people with any necessary vegetable product. Would he lay out hundreds of thousands of small tracts, scattered from Maine to California, or would he select the most desirable locations as to soil and climate adapted to the product, and there produce the required amount? Is it not true that the latter process would be the more economical, therefore the more desirable? Is it not true that the fundamental principle of progress is to produce the required amount of necessary products with the least amount of labor, thus leaving the mind and body free to labor for the greatest time possible in the field of actual progress,— that of improvement on present methods? If you acknowledge this much, you must accept the idea of a central city and the control of the field of production by the people; for it is the logical conclusion of greatest economy in production, under which system individual labor is reduced to minimum requirements, and the freedom of the individual in the path of inclination is secured for its maximum time.

THE INDUSTRIAL SYSTEM.

Up to the present, the reader's attention has only been directed to the inanimate machine of this new civilization. As yet, you probably have no conception as to how it is to be kept in motion, or how the necessary manual labor that must form a part of its ponderous moving mechanism is to be supplied without discord or unnecessary friction.

The labor necessary to this system of material equality and centralization would be reduced to a minimum point of economy, and it has been calculated that a force not to exceed ten per cent. of our population would be quite sufficient to meet every demand of material welfare. This would include all the labor incident to raw production, manufacture, distribution, preparing and dispensing of food, extension and maintenance of "Metropolis," general extension of public improvements, etc. It would be found that ten per cent. of our population could be maintained by employing all men and women between the age of twenty-five and thirty years. In other words, there are at the present time in the United States, about seven million human beings, whose ages range from twenty-five to thirty years ; and with the natural increase of population there would be a proportionate increase of numbers between twenty-five and thirty years of age. Therefore, if we make it compulsory for every man and woman to enter the service of the people at the age of twenty-five, there to remain until they are thirty, we could maintain the required working force continuously. But a difficulty arises here, which at first thought appears unsurmountable : How are we going to distribute this enormous working force through the various branches of industry, and avoid dissatisfaction and discord? I will tell you. In my opinion there is only one way this can be done. Each individual must be allowed to select his or her own vocation in the public service. But here another difficulty arises. Some branches of the public service would have more applicants than could be employed, while others would fall far short of necessary requirements. The reasons for this are plain. Some fields of labor are more desirable than others ; some are dangerous ; others are disagreeable ; while others are necessary hardships. These and many other reasons would result in the overcrowding of some departments of public service, while others would go begging for applicants. We can only overcome this difficulty by a system which will equalize individual labor.

THE SYSTEM OF EQUALIZATION OF LABOR.

Under this system of equalization, a perfect equilibrium would be maintained in every branch of the public service. Demand and supply of labor would be perfectly balanced at all times, this balance being found in the sliding scale of days demanded in each particular service. Every branch of public service would be listed, and the number of days demanded would be placed opposite each service. From day to day, the number of days demanded for any particular service would rise and fall to meet the supply and demand in that particular department, in competition with all other departments. If, for some particular service, it was found that the supply of labor was not equal to the demand, the time demanded would be reduced; and thus labor in that particular department, in competition with other departments, would become more desirable, and begin to attract applicants for service. If, in other departments, it was found that supply was exceeding the demand for labor, then the days demanded in that department would increase until it became less desirable, thus turning the excess of applicants into other branches of public service. Thus no necessary employment would go begging for volunteers for service. If it was found at any time that there was a general shortage in the labor market, there would be a per cent. increase in time due throughout the whole list of labor, which, going into effect at once and affecting all of those then in the field of labor, would check the dropping out of those whose time was about to expire, and thus rapidly overcome any shortage. On the other hand, if there was a surplus of labor, there would be a per cent. decrease in time demanded.

The required age for entering service would be compulsory *more by established custom than law*, and in time demanded, would probably range from a few days to ten years, the shorter time being for particularly hazardous or disagreeable employments, for which applicants would be few; while the longer time would be for the less laborious and more agreeable employments, which could only be kept from overcrowding by raising time demanded to the highest limit it would stand. Between these two extremes, would range all the various employments, each rising and falling in time demanded to meet the requirements of the supply and demand of labor.

This is not only a perfect system of supply and demand of labor, but I think it is the only one whereby large aggregations of people can divide the necessary labor of production and distribution on a basis of just compensation, and under which each chooses his own field of occupation, thus leaving no room for the individual to complain of favoritism or injustice. Each having an equal opportunity to choose will naturally choose that vocation most favorable to him or her from their point of view.

Under this system, the time demanded in any single branch of public service is the exact equivalent of the time demanded in any other branch, no matter how widely they may be separated in actual time demanded. This system may be objected to by some on the plea that many would refuse to labor when their time came to enter service. This might be true if we had the present generation always to deal with; but, when we consider that twenty-five years will see ninety per cent. of those who are now over forty years of age "gone to that bourne from which no traveller returns," and their places filled by a larger number who have been born and educated under the new system of government, I think it will be conceded that it is impossible to contrast that future with the present. After twenty-five years, all who were doing compulsory labor under the new system would be those who had been born and educated under the new conditions. They would know no other system, and they would no more think of refusing to do their equivalent portion of labor than they would refuse to be educated. Having been taught from the beginning to look forward to this period of labor, they would enter upon their chosen work with pleasure.

Every individual would be held strictly to account for full time of service ; and, if during time of service a change were made from one branch of public service to another, the change could only be made on a basis of equalization.

Thus, if a man entered a service which demanded two thousand days, and should afterwards change to a service which demanded only one thousand days, allowance for time served would be on a basis of one day under new service for each two days under the old. No reduction would be allowed from time demanded for any cause except invalidism. Loss of time from temporary illness would not be deducted, but would be demanded at the end of the regular term of service ; for the individual debt to humanity could not be cancelled until equivalent of time demanded had been paid in full. At the expiration of this term of service, each individual would receive his or her diploma of exemption from further arbitrary labor except for a limited period of time after the individual had attained a mature age, when their services would be required in one of the many directing bureaus, for promoting the welfare of the people. Before and after the term of service, the individual would be free to follow the channel of his or her inclination, and be entitled to all the benefits of education and material prosperity.

It can readily be seen that under this system of employment, the general average of time required in all departments of public service would depend, as a whole, upon the economical or extravagant use of material by the people. This in itself would mitigate against the prodigal use or waste of the products or consumption.

The field of labor which we are now considering would be entirely distinct from the actual avenue of progress, inasmuch as it would only be the mechanical work of the mind or body under the directing power of directing bureaus, while the true avenue of progress would depend on the mind-conceptions of the whole people in the field of improvement; and we can readily believe that such improvement would be rapid in every branch of public welfare, when we consider that every human being would be educated and free to follow his or her own inclination throughout the greater part of life.

The question will naturally arise, Who will constitute the directing power of the field of labor, and how will they attain their position in the different bureaus? I will say that this question might be solved in two ways,—by voluntary offer of services at a required age or by arbitrary rule, as is the case in the employment of labor. The latter seems the more practical.

We will suppose that the man or woman has attained a required age of forty years, and that the time of service in some one directing bureau is compulsory for a given time, after which they can voluntarily continue that service or retire, and thereafter follow their own inclinations. Now, it would be natural to suppose that men and women who had arrived at this age under conditions of equality would be of mature judgment. They would have followed their channel of inclination for a period of from five to ten years since their exemption from arbitrary labor. This channel of inclination must of necessity have been connected with progress in some department of public welfare. As a result, they must be abreast of the times in that particular department. As there would be no difference in time demanded for service in the different bureaus, which need not exceed two years, it is only natural to suppose that each individual on reaching the required age of forty years, would attach himself or herself to that bureau where inclination directed, and many would continue their services years beyond the stipulated time. This system would obviate the necessity of elections, and remove the disturbing element of politics.

The labor of these bureaus would be wholly directing, the clerical work being a part of the field of labor. They would, in each instance, constitute a body similar to our present House of Representatives, and would direct the whole field of labor, and forward public improvements. To the respective bureaus, the people would present for adoption or rejection, their mind-conceptions of discovery or improvement in the field of science, art, and invention. In the event of acceptance, which would be a virtual acknowledgment of progress made, the individual would receive the credit due, no matter how little or great that step in advance might be. This would be duly recorded in his life record; and in addition he would receive either the circle, square, or the triangle, the circle being the highest recognition of merit that could be conferred, and to be secured only by a radical improvement or discovery of a great value. The square would be conferred for general improvements and inventions of merit. The triangle would be conferred for improvements in part, and for noticeable valuable services in the interests of the public. These three medals, while not constituting the incentive to ambition, would be ambition's acknowledged reward.

The bureaus would cover every avenue of public welfare. Among these would be the bureau of education, agriculture, architecture, manufacture, distribution, labor, transportation, electrical engineering, etc. Then, again, these bureaus would be divided and subdivided into technical parts; and these branches or parts would naturally come under the control of specialists, which would result in the highest ratio of progress.

I will not attempt to go into an elaborate description of the working of this system; for I believe the average intelligent reader has already set the machine in motion. They can see "Metropolis" with its beautiful buildings and immaculate cleanliness, while close at hand are centred the mighty mills and factories of commerce, pulsating with life; and radiating from this centre, the arteries of commerce that enter every field of production throughout the world.

The individual, having arrived at the prescribed age under this new civilization, appears before the Bureau of Labor. Here, he or she is presented with a list of every department of public service. Opposite each is noted the time demanded for that service. This list not only specifies the different departments of service; but every particular service in each department is accurately noted, so there will be no misunderstanding in regard to the labor required. Some branches of service would embrace a miscellaneous field of labor. For instance, in the field of agriculture a man might go from one field of production to another in rapid succession, thus being actively employed the greater part of the year. One week he might be kept planting wheat in Dakota, and the next week be gathering oranges in Florida, he being one of an army which was rapidly moved from one productive field to another, as demanded by the Bureau of Agriculture. In winter, he could be employed in Central America, Mexico, and the South; in the summer, in the Middle and Northern States and in Canada. The labor of a single individual under this system would be more than the equivalent of ten under the present system, which gives employment to the farmer for only a small portion of the year. Another great advantage under this system of agriculture would be the system of large bodies of individuals travelling together, which association would make the labor incident to agriculture a happy pastime,— a period of time which the rising generation would look forward to with pleasant anticipation; and, instead of shirking the responsibilities of labor, each would be anxious to pay his debt of obligation to humanity.

EDUCATION.

The first and most important industry of this new civilization would be to cultivate brains, from which it would hope to reap a continuous harvest of new and scientifically faithful ideas that would promote progress.

The Educational Bureau would consist of those who had made the problem of education a life study. From this bureau would emanate the system employed in the schools and lecture halls.

The educational system would consist of four grand divisions of learning : first, the primary, or kindergarten, system ; second, the preparatory, or basis of science, system ; third, the technical, or special science, system ; fourth, the universal and special technical science lecture system.

The first, or primary, system of education would be compulsory. It would be forwarded on the kindergarten plan of instruction, which is designed to attract the interest and amuse the child. Thus, by means of object-lessons, the gradual training of the outward senses of perception would afford the desired instruction without mental strain or fatigue of the child, and eventually lead the inquiring intelligence into a natural channel of thought and inclination. Instruction in this department would extend over a period of from three to five years, or until the child was about seven years old.

The second, or preparatory, department of instruction would also be compulsory, and would extend over a period of about eight years, or until the child was fifteen years old. This department of instruction would be designed to instruct the child in the basis of all sciences, and cover the rules and formula of the whole field of the exact sciences, such as natural philosophy, chemistry, anatomy, botany, astronomy, music, etc., until the child would be carried forward to a plane where it could dissect and analyze its environment as far as the exact rules of science would allow.

Compulsory education would be best up to this point, for this reason. It is more important to the public that the child should be educated to its highest working capacity, and thus become an instrument of progressive development, than it is to either the individual parent or child. To the public it means a benefit to all, inasmuch as it raises the standard of united intelligence, which is a higher moral view than simply benefit to the individual parent or child. For this reason, the public mind should look upon the education of the rising generation as of *first* and *greatest* importance in the establishment of an economic basis of progress ; for upon such development of individual intelligence depends the rapidity of our advance to a higher ideal.

The third and technical, or special science, system would not be compulsory. It is supposed that the child, after its completion of the preparatory course, would arrive at a plane of intelligence where the inquiring mind would find its greatest happiness in some department of learning to which it would be directed by natural inclination ; and the technical science system would be designed to carry him forward in any special study to the highest point of knowledge and speculation. The mental qualification of the individual to grasp a subject would be heightened by his desire of obtaining particular knowledge, which obviates the necessity of any regular system of instruction. So this department of educational system would be carried forward by an organized army of lecturers on special subjects. Lecture halls for this particular department of instruction would be found in every educational building in the city, and the public would be informed at all times of the subjects and places where delivered. Thus the public would have a continuous system of instruction beyond the regular compulsory system, which they could continue to take advantage of throughout their life. These lectures would be by specialists and lecturers of pronounced ability, and their lectures would be the most advanced ideas and knowledge on the subject in hand. When desirable for purposes of clear definition, these lectures could be illustrated pictorially, mechanically, or otherwise.

The number of lecture halls for forwarding these branches of special instruction would number not less than five in each educational building, or in the total number of such buildings, which has been placed at four thousand for our present population, there would be a total of twenty thousand such lecture halls, each capable of seating one thousand or more persons.

The period of compulsory labor would not necessarily be without advantages of instruction; for the individual would have, in a large measure, opportunities for attending these lectures, and, where this was not possible, the individual would have such complete knowledge of the rules of science that he would necessarily apply them in his mind to his surroundings. Thus he would become the inventor, the scientist, and the philosopher.

In connection with every institution of learning, would be a physical training school, which would be carried forward under defined rules of class instruction, in charge of professional athletes. This gymnasium department would begin with the child, and carry it forward to maturity by a gradual process of daily training that would keep pace with the training of the mind, which would give the individual complete control of his body in its every movement, develop the physical strength, and promote a healthful circulation. It is only by such training that the body can be made to act with the alertness of the mind, and accuracy in action can be brought to science.

This instruction would apply the same to women as to men, and would result in the development of a race that would be physically strong, healthful, beautiful, and graceful.

THE BUREAU OF FOOD PREPARATION.

From this bureau would emanate those who would have charge of the culinary departments,— professors who were scientific experts in the preparation of food products for the table, men and women who had made the combinations and cooking of food a study, who knew the chemical properties of every food product, and the chemical changes resulting from their combination with other products. Under these professors who would superintend special divisions of food preparation, the preparing of food would become a science.

The labor element of the culinary departments would be a part of the field labor, and supplied under the system of equalization, which has been described.

These departments of "Metropolis" would be maintained on the grandest and most liberal scale, and on the most economical use of labor. We have four thousand of these departments, contributing to twenty-four thousand apartment houses. Each of these would be presided over by specialists in every separate department of food preparation, and under the directions of each professor would be a necessary corps of assistants who prepared the food.

These culinary department buildings would cover the same ground space as the apartment houses, and in larger part consist of store and refrigerating rooms. All food products, such as fruits and vegetables, which are supposed to be consumed almost as soon as gathered, would be sent in trainloads direct from the fields of production to a distributing warehouse, which would be some miles in extent, and lie just on the outskirts of the city. Here it would be divided, and thence delivered, over electric roads in automatically controlled electric cars, to the various departments; and the menu from day to day would embrace every food product which might be in season, and the limitless combinations possible in their preparation. All products of a non-perishable nature, or which could be kept for future use, would be delivered in quantity to last for a month or a year; and the storerooms would be kept at the desired temperatures to insure best results, by an automatic system of heating and refrigeration.

Under this system such a thing as adulteration would be unknown. From the first preparation of ingredients to their final combination, they would each be superintended by specialists. The highest standard of quality would always be maintained; special and scientific intelligence would be brought to bear on each separate article of diet, and public recognition of genius and progress in this department of material welfare would be as readily accorded as in other scientific departments.

We would have in "Metropolis" about four thousand kitchens and twenty-four thousand dining apartments, from which sixty million people would be served daily with every food product the world could produce, all food being prepared by a scientific formula. How would this compare, in point of economy, with our present system of not less than fifteen million individual kitchens, many with their ignorant housewives or servants, with their outfit of stoves, ranges, and cooking utensils, and many women obliged to do their own work, and live in perpetual slavery and anxiety from day to day? Not one in fifty of these women know the first rudiments of preparing palatable and wholesome food. They are limited in materials and means to a few simple articles of diet of a coarse nature. Many of them do not pretend to purchase first-class material, for they cannot afford it.

The kitchens of "Metropolis," six hundred feet in diameter, would be as light as day and as white as snow, and immaculate in their cleanliness ; for they would be porcelain-finish throughout.

Under such a system, the servant question would be solved, and highest intelligence would take the place of ignorance in the preparation and serving of food.

THE BUREAU OF VITAL STATISTICS.

The Bureau of Vital Statistics, for many reasons, would be one of the most important branches of this United People. This bureau at all times would constitute a complete genealogical record of each individual, and of the whole race under its jurisdiction, both past and present.

By the establishment of this bureau, we would be enabled at any time to tell exactly what the population was, its proportion of males and females, how many there would be of any given age, and how many would arrive at the required age of service within a given time.

The first duty of the parent would be to place on record, in this bureau, the birth of any child ; and all deaths would be likewise recorded. Thus from day to day this record would be maintained in volumes expressly designed for this purpose. These volumes would be serially numbered, and the year, month, and day plainly lettered upon their back. Each child, in the order of its birth, would be given a consecutive birth number, which consecutive number would be a page in one of the volumes.

To more fully appreciate this system, we will take down an imaginary volume from the Historical Records of Vital Statistics. Each volume contains one thousand names. On the back of this volume we read : —

VOLUME NO. 187,543.

YEAR, 1934.

MONTH, MAY.

By turning to page 865 we find the following Life Record : —

Birth number.— 187,543,865.

Male child, name.— EDWARD GRANT.

Born.— Metropolis, May 25, 1934.

Father.— JOHN GRANT, birth number 107,890,411, born July 16, 1907.

Mother.— MARY GRANT, *née* MORGAN, birth number 102,332,506, born April 22, 1905.

Married.— Metropolis, Oct. 12, 1960.

Wife.— ALICE WORTHINGTON, birth number 191,282,541.

Children.—

ALFRED, birth number 232,955,823, born Jan. 5, 1962 ;
GEORGE, birth number 257,421,868, born Jan. 11, 1964;
MARGARET, birth number 291,866,349, born Dec. 16, 1967.

Photographs.— (Taken every fifth year during life.)

Life Record.— Inventor and mechanical engineer. Honorable mention in connection with improvements in the construction of elevators in public buildings, March 6, 1962. Specification and plans for utilization of the power of Niagara Falls, submitted in open competition with seven thousand six hundred and forty-two competitors ; accepted by the Bureau of Engineers, Nov. 30, 1977, for which honor he was presented with the highest tribute to be conferred by an appreciative public,— the Circle Number 862.

Member of the Bureau of Engineering from May 25, 1974, until his death.

Died.— April 17, 2005. Age, 71 years, 10 months, and 24 days.

Obituary.— Edward Grant was without a peer in his particular field of observation and labor, and substantial evidence of his originality and genius is found scattered throughout the country, to attest his worth and the indebtedness of the public to his untiring zeal in its behalf. Many honors were due him from the public since the highest honor, the circle, was conferred upon him ; but he refused them all, seemingly content with pleasure derived from labor and the approbation of his friends and associates.

As a writer upon engineering and philosophical subjects, he has contributed much that is new and of permanent value to our knowledge of power and its application. His essays upon the "Transference of Energy," and "The Oneness of Power in all Motion, and its Relation to Gravity," are used extensively in our schools, and have opened up a wide field of speculation that seems to have a close relation to future progress. Liberal in his ideas and generous in conferring credit to his associates, he won the respect and admiration of all with whom he came in contact.

He leaves two children to mourn his death ; and he will live for years to come, in the memory of loving friends and an appreciative people.

It can be readily seen that there is no break in this life record of the Bureau of Vital Statistics. Every individual can trace both branches of his family to the foundation of the system, and thus have a connected historical record of his ancestors, which would solve many of the problems of heredity. Further, this system would be invaluable in its relation to the supply and demand of labor ; for it would tell to a day when individuals had arrived at the required age of labor, for in the same consecutive order that individuals are born would they arrive at the required age, and be called upon to enter the field of labor. Again, it would be valuable as a statistical record of health and general average of life. From day to day the births would be added to the total of population, and the deaths would be subtracted. Thus at all times there would be a perfect knowledge of total population. The residence of every individual would be known, and change recorded with every change of residence.

Altogether, this Bureau of Vital Statistics would be the most important of all bureaus in its relation to historical progress ; for here could be traced, step by step, every forward movement of the human race, individually and collectively.

After the family record come twenty small spaces. In these spaces, beginning at the age of five years, and every five years thereafter, is placed a photograph of the individual whose life record is there recorded. Thus it will be seen that an individual living to the age of Edward Grant, whose life record is here given, would have fourteen photographs recorded on his page. The taking and recording of these photographs would be a special branch of the Bureau of Vital Statistics, and would constitute a valuable addition to the records of the bureau, as well as a valuable source of reference for every individual in the study of family history.

THE BUREAU OF HORTICULTURE.

The Bureau of Horticulture would consist of those who made this particular field a scientific study. On this bureau would devolve the intellectual labor of directing and maintaining the floral setting on which "Metropolis" would largely depend for its beauty and freshness, and evidence of life and perpetual care. The actual labor demanded for this work, aside from the directing power, would be maintained by the system of equalization of labor which has been described, and would require not less than five hundred thousand men and women employed throughout the year,— about one per cent. of the population.

All the soil used would be prepared and brought to the city. Large trees and plants would be set in immense pots which would be flanged on the outer upper edge. These pots would set down through the pavement, on which the flange would rest. Thus every walk would be lined with trees on their outer edges and through their centres, and around these trees would be artistic seats. An automatic system of watering and draining would insure the lasting greenness and freshness of grass and foliage for a longer time than if dependent on nature alone.

Around each building would be a lawn one hundred and fifty feet in width, and more than half a mile in length on its outer circumference, artistically laid out with trees, shrubs, and beds of flowers.

There would be thirty-six thousand conservatories, each a separate work of art, covering more than an acre in extent, combining all the rare and beautiful trees, plants, and flowers that the world could produce; artificial grottos and fountains of fantastic and beautiful designs. In addition to this, every dining-room would be an artistic inspiration in its floral display; and every railing which encircled the different 'andings in the interior courts of buildings would have, at regular intervals, beautiful urns of flowers.

Can any one say that such an ideal is not possible? Flowers can be multiplied to infinity; and no city can be perfect without such an ideal setting. Flowers are nature's truest expression of grace and beauty; and no one can approximate in imagination what the reality would be under social material equality, where all were equally desirous to make the environment appeal to our highest sense of the beautiful. Can such an ideal ever be attained under our present system of competition for material wealth? Never! for individual effort can never reach the plane of united intelligence. Under competition for individual wealth, individual effort is wholly selfish; and, even though an individual had an ideal conception of what was thought perfection, he could not carry it out. *On the other hand, united intelligence, once in control, would command the whole field of production and distribution, and direct every change, and demand highest attainable perfection in every avenue of progress.*

I shall not further attempt to describe this new civilization. Other bureaus, which would cover every branch of material welfare, would maintain their necessary complement of laborers by the system of equalization of labor; and the system would be just and equable. The aggregate amount of labor employed at any one time would depend on the material wants of the people as a whole, and the equalized amount of time that each individual would labor would also depend on the material wants of the people; but the advance made in labor-saving devices and machinery would rapidly reduce the aggregate amount of labor required for a given amount of product.

CONCLUSION.

It is my firm belief that under conditions of material equality, all necessary labor could be forwarded without friction; that a system of compensation to balance supply and demand for labor, carried out on plan proposed, could be reduced to an exact science, and humanity would march along the highway of progress without any disturbing elements to check its advance. The business of production and distribution, which now demands at least ninety per cent. of all the brain power of the world, and is almost the sole subject of conversation between individuals, and, either awake or sleeping, draws upon the mind's vitality, would no longer occupy the attention of the people. The whole channel of conversation and thought would be turned, as if by magic, into the field of scientific research and improvement in invention and devices for production that would save manual labor and increase the quantity and quality of products. Thus the world would gain what is now an enormous waste of brain power, which would be devoted to the field of progress in science, art, and invention; and our rapid advance to a higher ideal would be in proportion to this gain. The thoughts and conversation would no longer turn to wealth and production, for production and distribution would be mechanical, based on our progressive position; and to advance this progressive position would be the field of competition, and demand all thought and conversation.

Except those who were in the field of labor, the people would be free to follow their own inclination. Having contributed their share of labor, they would have earned their right to all the benefits of progress. There would be no restrictions whatever on their actions, and they could go and come with absolute freedom. They could travel or stay at home, study or be idle, eat and drink what they pleased, and at any place or hour that suited their convenience.

With the absence of poverty and crime, and the anxiety, worry, and care incident to our present system of competition, disease and sickness would rapidly disappear; and, with equal advantages of education and freedom, genius would crop out in the mind and features of every individual, and *the conscious law of right would be the guide to every action.*

Do I hear some of my readers say that with so much time at the disposal of the masses, we should become a dissipated or idle race? If so, I must differ with your judgment of humanity; for, under these favorable conditions of environment, the mind would be compelled to follow some channel of progress, or the individual would be at an absolute loss in his association with his fellow-men, for science would then occupy all thought and conversation, the same as money and its attainment now occupy almost all thought and conversation.

Such a city and such a civilization as I have described could be forwarded and brought to a successful conclusion within the lifetime of many now living, but the reality would be so far ahead of my power of description that I have hesitated to approach this part of the subject at all. In this description, I have confined myself in application to present knowledge in the field of science and invention, and have not attempted to soar into the possibilities of future discoveries, or the new application of present knowledge to a perfectly constructed machine. I have only described what is possible with our present knowledge, and used those materials which are within our knowledge and have common use. I have endeavored to describe a system that combines organization and economy, as opposed to our present system of disorganization and extravagance. I have not soared into the development of art and music, which would be the pastime and pleasure of the people as a whole, and would necessarily elevate the mass of humanity to a plane of refinement that would be beyond present conception.

I do not wish my readers to mistake me, and think that I am looking for any change that would be paramount to a miracle. I am altogether too conscious of the low moral plane of humanity to delude myself with any such belief, but we could reasonably expect that with the cause of crime (competition for material wealth) removed, crime itself would gradually disappear; for civilization, under these conditions of equal opportunity, would be as full of life as a boiling cauldron, and all its dirt and filth would gradually rise to the top and disappear, leaving naught but minds of crystal purity behind. It would result in a civilization strong, honest, and just. Though bound together by bonds of common interest, men would stand separate and apart in their individuality, and minds would only coalesce in passing judgment on individual conceptions. Thus would humanity, in its material welfare, always keep pace with highest individual conceptions, finding expression in action by united intelligence. Never can man hope to attain a high development of intelligence and virtue until material equality is secured and organization takes the place of competition for material wealth.

As a last and fitting close to this subject, I wish to once more impress my readers with the truth of my conclusions.

1st. That economy in production is the very essence of progress.

2d. That any system of production and distribution which has the economical power to displace another is superior to the system displaced.

3d. The system advocated in this volume has the economical power to displace our present system, and is therefore superior to it.

4th. It is not a question for argument as to how such change will affect individuals, but to find out how it will affect society as a whole,— the individual will be compelled to adjust himself to any change that may result.

5th. If it is possible for one individual or one corporation to control one line of product, it is possible for the people, as a whole, to control the whole field of production and distribution. By gradual absorption, this is possible ; for from start to finish it would be but the perfecting of a machine of which we would never lose control.

My friends, this is not politics ; it is not religion. It is hard-pan common business sense. There need be no difference of opinion to keep you apart : all would be equally benefited by the change. I appeal to your better nature (which is an integral part of every human mind) to come together in this common cause of humanity. Come, you who are rich, powerful, and influential, and you who are poor, and broken from unceasing toil. Come one, come all, and join the ranks of an overwhelming United People's Party. Let us start the ball rolling with such a boom and enthusiasm that it will draw the wealth and sinew of the nation into its vortex,— the great future city " Metropolis." Such a city and such a system of production and distribution would be like a living, breathing creation in the automatic working and perfect unison of its mechanism, whose soul would be the combined intelligence of man. It would be something to love, for it would always represent a perfect reflection of man's effort to reach the ideal.

Let us tear asunder the chrysalis which binds within its folds the intellect of man, and let the polar star of every thought find its light in nature's truths. Forward ! is the cry. " Let the dead past bury its dead," and let a new era of civilization and progress shed its light of hope on the future of mankind.